Bible Rap

Stephen Amato

Copyright © 2003 by Stephen Amato

Bible Rap
by Stephen Amato

Printed in the United States of America

Library of Congress Control Number: 2003101812
ISBN 1-591605-17-2

All rights reserved. No part of this publication may be reproduced or transmitted in any form or by any means without written permission of the publisher.

Unless otherwise indicated, Bible quotations are taken from The World English Bible. Copyright © 2003 by Rainbow Missions, Inc.

Xulon Press
10640 Main Street
Fairfax, VA 22030
(703) 934-4411
XulonPress.com

To order additional copies,
call 1-866-909-BOOK (2665).

Dedication

In dedication to God the Father
and the Lord Jesus Christ, to whom be all glory,
honor and praise.

Preface

The Bible rap contained in this book is supplemental to the Bible study guides I've written for the Boston Christian Bible Study Resources site (http://www.bcbsr.com) From my perspective, the vast majority of teaching materials available and techniques utilized in the Evangelical community today speak mostly to those of a left-brain analytic mindset, of which I myself am no doubt a member. But all kinds of people are to be invited to the feast. How to invite someone of an artistic intuitive nature to feast on the Word? This book is an attempt to minister to one's artistic and intuitive nature while attempting to keep to the accuracy and depth of the Word of God and the meaning of the Christian experience.

> Once there was a man who found a treasure.
> Hidden in a field, and he took pleasure.
> In selling all he had to buy that field.
> To gain the treasure it would yield.
> God has a treasure, it's hidden away.

> But seek and you shall find some day.
> That treasure he offers which is life through the Son.
> A life which will last after your life here is done.

In the last section of this book, the section on "Becoming a Christian," though I use illustrations, I divert from the poetic forms to speak more directly on the subject of entering the Kingdom of God.

Now as I desire for readers to feel free to utilize this material as they feel led, I the author allow this material to be utilized free from copyright restrictions. Use it as you wish. And may the grace of the Lord Jesus be with you.

Stephen Amato

Contents

The Parables of Jesus xi

Parable Raps 21
   Lamp Under a Basket 21
   A Wise Man's Foundation 22
   New Cloth on and Old Garment 22
   New Wine in Old Wineskins............................23
   The Sower 23
   The Wheat and the Weeds 24
   The Mustard Seed 25
   The Leaven...25
   The Hidden Treasure..26
   The Pearl of Great Price 26
   The Dragnet..27
   The Householder..27
   The Lost Sheep 28
   The Unforgiving Servant..................................28
   The Workers in the Vineyard 30
   The Two Sons...31
   The Wicked Tenants...31

Bible Rap

The Wedding Feast 32
The Fig Tree 33
The Ten Virgins 34
The Talents 35
The Growing Seed 36
The Watchful Porter 37
The Creditor and Two Debtors 37
The Good Samaritan 38
A Friend in Need 39
The Rich Fool 40
The Faithful and Wise Servant 41
The Faithful and Wicked Steward 42
The Barren Fig Tree 43
The Lowest Seat 43
Building a Tower and Making War 44
The Lost Coin 45
The Lost Son 45
The Shrewd Manager 47
The Rich Man and Lazarus 49
The Unworthy Servants 50
The Persistent Widow 51
The Pharisee and the Tax Collector 51

Isaiah 53 Rap—The Suffering Messiah 53
John 17 Rap –A Prayer of Jesus 57
Apologetics Rap 61
Song of Redemption 65
1John Rap 69
James Rap 83
1Peter Rap 93
2Peter Rap 105
Becoming a Christian 113

The Parables of Jesus Christ

	Parable	Matthew	Mark	Luke
1	Lamp Under a Basket	5:14-16	4:21,22	8:16,17
				11:33-36
2	A Wise Man's Foundation	7:24-27	.	6:47-49
3	New Cloth on and Old Garment	9:16	2:21	5:36
4	New Wine in Old Wineskins	9:17	2:22	5:37,38
5	The Sower	13:3-23	4:2-20	8:4-15
6	The Wheat and the Weeds	13:24-30	.	.
7	The Mustard Seed	13:31,32	4:30-32	13:18,19
8	The Leaven	13:33	.	13:20,21
9	The Hidden Treasure	13:44	.	.
10	The Pearl of Great Price	13:45,46	.	.
11	The Dragnet	13:47-50	.	.
12	The Householder	13:52	.	.
13	The Lost Sheep	18:12-14	.	15:3-7
14	The Unforgiving Servant	18:23-35	.	.
15	The Workers in the Vineyard	20:1-16	.	.
16	The Two Sons	21:28-32	.	.
17	The Wicked Tenants	21:33-45	12:1-12	20:9-19
18	The Wedding Feast	22:2-14	.	14:16-24
19	The Fig Tree	24:32-44	13:28-32	21:29-33
20	The Ten Virgins	25:1-13	.	.
21	The Talents	25:14-30	.	.
22	The Growing Seed	.	4:26-29	.
23	The Watchful Porter	.	13:33-37	.
24	The Creditor and Two Debtors	.		7:41-43
25	The Good Samaritan	.		10:30-37
26	A Friend in Need	.		11:5-13
27	The Rich Fool	.		12:16-21
28	The Faithful and Wise Servant			12:35-40
29	Faithful and Wicked Steward	24:45-51		12:42-48
30	The Barren Fig Tree			13:6-9
31	The Lowest Seat			14:7-11
32	Building a Tower and Making War			14:25-35
33	The Lost Coin			15:8-10
34	The Lost Son			15:11-32
35	The Shrewd Manager			16:1-13
36	The Rich Man and Lazarus			16:19-31
37	Unprofitable Servants			17:7-10
38	The Persistent Widow			18:1-8
39	The Pharisee and the Tax Collector			18:9-14
40	The Minas (Pounds)			19:11-27

Parable Topics

Entry into God's Kingdom

God's Concern for the Lost

<u>Lost Sheep</u> Matt 18:12-14; Lk 15:3-7
God's primary concern is for those who stray

<u>Lost Coin</u> Lk 15:8-10
God rejoices over the repentance of one sinner

<u>Lost Son</u> Lk 15:11-32
All who repent are heirs of God's forgiving grace without distinction.

Prerequisite Attitudes to Enter God's Kingdom

Placing Value on Eternal Things

The Wedding Feast Matt 22:2-14; Lk 14:16-24
Though many are invited to partake of eternal life, few respond and many have trivial excuses.

Hidden Treasure Matt 13:44
Saving faith has the quality of valuing the kingdom above all

The Pearl of Great Price Matt 13:45,46
Total commitment to the kingdom should be given because of its infinite worth

The Rich Fool Lk 12:16-21
The faith that saves is one that looks to eternal rewards rather than earthly material things

Humility

Pharisee and the tax collector Lk 18:9-14
God's forgiveness comes to the repentant, not the self-righteous

Application Oriented Faith

A Wise Man's Foundation Matt 7:24-27; Lk 6:47-49
Obedience to the word of God provides a strong foundation for salvation

Entry Into God's Kingdom

<u>Two Sons</u> Matt 21:28-32
Reluctant obedience is more acceptable that fake obedience.
The "irreligious" Jew who repents will enter the kingdom rather than the unfaithful Jewish leaders.

Commitment

<u>Building a Tower and a King Making War</u> Lk 14:25-35
Only after one has counted the cost should he say that he believes

Forgiveness

<u>Unmerciful Servant</u> Matt 18:23-35
If you do not forgive in the manner that God forgave you, neither will you be forgiven.

Sufficient Information to Enter God's Kingdom

<u>Rich Man and Lazarus</u> Lk 16:19-31
The Word of God contains sufficient information to persuade people into the kingdom apart from their personal experience of miracles.

<u>The Growing Seed</u> Mk 4:26-29
God will bring about His kingdom apart from human effort

Nominalism—False Believers

<u>The Weeds</u> Matt 13:24-30; 36-43
Until the judgment day, it may be difficult to distinguish between real and nominal Christians within the kingdom of God.

<u>The Mustard Seed</u> Matt 13:31,32; Mk 4:30-32; Lk 13:18,19
Though the kingdom begins small, it will be large at the end.
And non-Christians will nest in its branches.

<u>The Leaven</u> Matt 13:33; Lk 13:20,21
Nominalism grows quickly in the Kingdom

<u>The Dragnet</u> Matt 13:47-50
Though many enter into Christendom, they will be separated on Judgment day.

What about Israel & Judaism?

Attitude Towards the Old Covenant

<u>New Cloth on an Old Garment</u> Matt 9:16; Mk 2:21; Lk 5:36
<u>New Wine in Old Wineskins</u> Matt 9:17; Mk 2:22; Lk 5:37,38
Righteousness by faith is independent of the Law of Moses

Judgment upon unbelieving Israel

<u>Tenants</u> Matt 21:33-45; Mk 12:1-12; Lk 20:9-19
In the present age God has transferred stewardship of His kingdom from unbelieving Israel to other stewards

The Christian Walk

Application of God's Word

<u>The Householder</u> Matt 13:52
Disciples should be able to draw spiritual truths and applications from the Jesus' teachings.

Serving God—Obedience

<u>Ten Minas</u> Lk 19:11-27
Disciples of Jesus are to remain faithful until He returns

<u>Talents</u> Matt 25:14-30
One must be prepared for the coming of Christ by commitment to service

<u>Unworthy Servants</u> Lk 17:7-10
Disciples are not to expect gratitude for everything they do;
Service must come from a sense of duty

Fruitfulness

The Sower Matt 13:3-23; Mk 4:2-20; Lk 8:4-15
Productivity within the kingdom depends on the kind of response to the Word one makes.

Barren Fig Tree Lk 13:6-9
God will bring judgment on those who produce no fruitfulness to God

Money

Shrewd Manager Lk 16:1-13
Christians should develop mastery over material things in service to God.

Love

Good Samaritan Lk 10:30-37
Christian love is to provide for the needs of others impartially

Gratitude of the Redeemed

The Creditor and the Two Debtors Lk 7:41-43
Gratitude for forgiveness is proportionate to the recognition of one's sinfulness.

Workers in the Vineyard Matt 20:1-16
Christians should not be envious of the graciousness that God shows to others.

The Light of the Redeemed

Lamp Under a Basket Matt 5:14-16; Mk 4:21,22; Lk 8:16,17; Lk 11:33-36
Christians should promote rather than suppress the truth

Humility

Lowest seat at the feast Lk 14:7-11
Disciples are to be exalted by God, not by themselves

Persistence in Prayer

Friend at midnight Lk 11:5-13
If a neighbor will certainly help in time of need rather than bring shame on himself, how much more will God meet the needs of those who ask

Persistent Widow Lk 18:1-8
If an unjust judge will give justice because of persistence, how much more will the just and gracious God make things right at the coming of Christ.

Christ's Return and the Final Judgment

The Faithful and Wise Servant Lk 12:35-40
The faith that saves is one that looks to the return of the master

The Fig Tree Matt 24:32-44; Mk 13:28-32; Lk 21:29:33
There will be signs of Christ's coming available for Christians.

The Ten Virgins Matt 25:1-13
Those who intend to meet Christ at His return must be prepared in view of the imminence of His coming.

Wise and Wicked Servants Matt 24:45-51; Lk 12:42-48
All true followers of Jesus will watch and be ready for His return.

Watchful Porter Mk 13:33-37
True followers of Jesus will watch and be ready for His return.

Parable Raps

The Parable of a Lamp Under a Basket

Matt 5:14-16; Mk 4:21,22; Lk 8:16,17;
Lk 11:33-36

Who puts a lamp under a bed?
Doesn't he put it on a stand instead?
For there's nothing hid that will not be revealed
All will be known which once was concealed.
Your eye is a lamp, even at night.
When your eye is good, your body is light.
But if your eye is bad, your body is dark.
your behavior corrupt and your heart like rock.
But if you open your heart to the light of the Lord
You will with Him be of one accord.

The Parable of A Wise Man's Foundation

Matt 7:24-27; Lk 6:47-49

Let me tell you of one who does what I say
He digs down deep, a foundation to lay
Upon the rock his house will stand
Amidst the torrent and Satan's hand.
But the one who doesn't do what I say
Will not be prepared for that day.
If you build your house on the sand
It will be washed from the land
All your works will be destroyed
And God's wrath you can't avoid.

The Parable of New Cloth on an Old Garment

Matt 9:16; Mk 2:21; Lk 5:36

No one tears a patch from a brand new set of clothes
And sews it on an old one, for everybody knows
They end up being ruined the ones which are new
And neither will the patch match the old one too
The Law had its purpose and now it is fulfilled
It brought conviction of our sin
which is what God willed
But now by grace we're saved
through faith we cannot ask for more
Let's not tear apart that grace to be justified by law.

Parable Raps

The Parable of New Wine in Old Wineskins

Matt 9:17; Mk 2:22; Lk 5:37,38

If in old skins you put new wine
Not what is aged, but straight from the vine
The skins will burst and the wine run out
That is, if you keep the cork in the snout.
New wine must be put into new skins
To store the wine as fermenting begins
And no one after drinking the old
Says the new is better, so I'm told
Thus the Jews rejected God's grace
For an empty old skin in its place.

The Parable of The Sower

Matt 13:3-23; Mk 4:2-20; Lk 8:4-15

One day a farmer went out to sow
Scattering seed to and fro
Some fell along the path
Which could not deliver from God's wrath
For the devil took what they hadn't craved
So they didn't believe and were not saved.
Some fell on rocks but withered and died
For their faith was not deep enough to be qualified
To receive the life God promised to those
Who really believed Jesus died and arose.
Yes at first they were overjoyed
But when trials came their faith was destroyed
For they received it without their faith being rooted

Bible Rap

And so fell away after they were persecuted
But then some among thorns fell
But in the end didn't mature too well.
For they were too concerned for their security
To bring any fruit to maturity
But those on good soil retained what they heard
It wasn't taken away by any bird
Nor did they fall away like those on the rock
But continued to believe when others did mock
The problems in life would not make them stop
And by persevering they produced a crop

The Parable of The Wheat and the Weeds

Matt 13:24-30; 36-43

The kingdom is like a man who had sown
Wheat in his field to reap after it's grown
But while still seed an enemy came
To sow weeds in the field that looked quite the same
The man's servant offered to pull the weeds out
But he might pull the wheat just as it sprout
No, safer to let the two grow together
And in harvest to reap in just the right weather
Put the wheat in the barn, tie the weeds to be burned.
Now let us consider what lesson we learned.
Jesus is sowing his seed on the earth
But the weeds are the ones whom the devil gave birth.
Difficult at times to distinguish the two,
Between a false Christian and one who is true.
When they are young they have only roots.
But you shall know them by their fruits.

The weeds will not last, they will be thrown out
Into a furnace in anguish no doubt.
But the righteous will shine just like the Son.
But of these two seeds, you are which one?

The Parable of The Mustard Seed

Matt 13:31,32; Mk 4:30-32; Lk 13:18,19

The kingdom is like a mustard seed
Small at first but it did succeed
To grow with branches far and wide
Onto which birds did abide

The visible church started quite small
But popular today with buildings quite tall
But beware of the birds that nest in its branches
who take advantage of the circumstances

The Parable of The Leaven

Matt 13:33; Lk 13:20,21

There once was some dough without any leaven
Just like the bread that came down from heaven
But then a woman added yeast to the dough
False teachings and malice made it grow
Being bloated with pride and full of hot air
So when you see such yeast, beware
For sincerity and truth is the bread without yeast
And so with such bread let us keep the feast

Bible Rap

The Parable of The Hidden Treasure

Matt 13:44

Once there was a man who found a treasure
Hidden in a field, and he took pleasure
In selling all he had to buy that field
To gain the treasure it would yield
God has a treasure, it's hidden away
But seek and you shall find some day
That treasure he offers which is life through the Son
A life which will last after your life here is done

The Parable of The Pearl of Great Price

Matt 13:45,46

There once was a merchant looking for pearls
Thinking of them like nuts to squirrels
But one day he found a pearl of great price
And sold all he had, all his merchandise
To buy the pearl he sought the most
Which in the end would be his boast.
There are those who seek from place to place
What can be found only through God's grace
The pearl of great price is Jesus our Lord
When you find Him you'll find that you can afford
To replace your trust in other things
With the One from whom eternal life springs

The Parable of The Dragnet

Matt 13:47-50

A fisherman threw his net in the lake
And caught all kinds of fish, both true and fake
For the net is the gospel that draws both kind
And in this age they are confined
To dwell together in the visible church
But in the end the angels will search
To take the wicked from the good
To be thrown into hell as they should
So if you are sure you are saved
'cause you go to church, but aren't well-behaved
You will be judged by what you do
For there are Christians both false and true.
But the false will end up underneath
Where there will be weeping and gnashing of teeth.

The Parable of The Householder

Matt 13:51

Teachers who know both the kingdom and the Law
Instructed in the truth can upon such knowledge draw
Like a master of a house
bringing out old things and new
To instruct the humble student
in all things which are true.
Both testaments have value both new and the old
For God's Word is eternal and also manifold
But as we read the Bible making observations

Bible Rap

Let us by our spirit infer the applications

The Parable of The Lost Sheep

Matt 18:12-14; Lk 15:3-7

Suppose you owned a hundred sheep
And one wandered away when you fell asleep
Wouldn't you leave the rest to find
The one that left. Aren't you inclined
To seek the one that you own
Though you must leave the rest alone
And when you find the sheep off track
What would you do to get him back?
Would you simply hand him a map?
Or perhaps you might try and give him a slap.
No, you would lift him right off his feet
And carry him home all the way down the street.
Rejoicing all the way you go.
Just as God's angels do, you know.
For there is more rejoicing over one who repents
Than over those who simply stayed in the fence

The Parable of The Unforgiving Servant

Matt 18:23-35

There once was a king wanting to settle accounts
With his servants and calculated all the amounts
These servants owed to the king in question
His demand for repayment was more than a suggestion

Parable Raps

There was a servant who owed him quite alot
But could he repay? No, he could not
So the master demanded all his things be sold
He and his family, his silver and gold
Then the servant fell to his knees
Hoping his master to appease
"Be patient with me. I know that I lack.
But if you wait, the debt I'll pay back."
The master took pity on him, you know
And cancelled his debt and let him go
But the servant then went out and found a fellow man
Who owed him just a little—grabbed him and began
To choke the fellow servant demanding he be paid.
But the servant fell to his knees trembling and afraid
"I will pay you back everything I owe.
Please just wait a while. Don't take this as a 'no'"
But the servant was impatient
and threw him into jail.
But word got to the king of this horrid tale.
And called the wicked servant in before his throne
"I forgave, you should too, this should have known.
But now you have revealed your real attitude
And so I am removing all your latitude."
He threw him into jail to pay back all he owed.
Being tortured day and night even after growing old.
This kind of treatment my Father will impart.
If you don't forgive your brothers
and do it from your heart

Bible Rap

The Parable of The Workers in the Vineyard

Matt 20:1-16

There once was a man who owned a vineyard
And needed some men to work very hard
He hired some men early in the day
And told them a denarius would be their pay
And every few hours he hired more men
Telling them the same again and again
Then in the evening he gave them their wage
But the ones who came early expressed outrage
"We worked harder than anyone here.
Aren't you being just a bit unfair."
"I'm not being unfair to you.
A denarius was what you agreed to."
Now take your pay and go.
Even though you thinks it's low.
For I'll be gracious to whom I want.
I'll be generous even though you aren't.
For many are victims of circumstance.
And hiring you early was a matter of chance.
There are Christians who live quite a long time.
Laboring all day taking care of the vine.
But some get saved after they are old
Or live a short while after entering the fold
But nonetheless on judgment day
Both may end up receiving the same pay
For the point is not simply doing his biz
But rather revealing how gracious he is.

The Parable of The Two Sons

Matt 21:28-32

A man had two sons and said to the one
Go work in the vineyard today my son
But the son at first just wouldn't obey
"I'm not going to work, no not today"
But later he changed his mind and went
Even though before he did not consent
He asked the second son the same
"Sir, I'll go" he did proclaim
But didn't go as he said he would
Though I'm sure he thought himself good.
Which of these two did his father's will
The first one did and the other did nil
Then Jesus spoke to the chief priest
And to the elders missing the feast
Those whom you think don't have a clue
Are entering the kingdom ahead of you
John showed you the way, you haven't believed
But sinners repented, his word they received
And after you saw how they did repent
You didn't really seem to care what he meant

The Parable of the Wicked Tenants

Matt 21:33-45; Mark 12:1-12; Luke 20:9-19

A man planted a vineyard which he did rent
To some tenants to care for, then he went
When harvest came he sent someone

Bible Rap

To get some fruit, but they gave none.
Another he sent, they beat and mistreated
And sent him away, but again he repeated
To send yet another, but they hurt and threw out
This made the owner quite angry no doubt
But wait I'll send my son to collect
The son whom I love they'll surely respect
But then the tenants took the son
And put him to death thinking they've won
But the owner came and killed those men
And gave the vineyard to others again.
The former treated the vineyard as if their own
But then they rejected the chief cornerstone
If you're in charge of part of God's churches
Don't be like a bird which on a branch perches
Thinking that he owns the whole tree
And eating its fruit as if it were free
For God owns the tree, you only rent.
And if you think different, you must repent.

The Parable of the Wedding Feast

Matt 22:2-14; Lk 14:16-24

The kingdom is like a king who prepared
A wedding feast for his son, and as the time neared
He sent out his servants to those he did invite.
To come to his feast and to bring their appetite
But they refused going back to their work
And some went so far as to go berserk
The servants they seized, mistreated and killed
The king was enraged and so he willed

Parable Raps

For those men to be killed and their city burned.
For that was really what they earned.
Then he told other servants to go all around
And invite anyone so that guests may be found
But when the king came in to see all of those
He noticed a man not wearing wedding clothes
How did you come in dressed that way?
The king asked the man but he had nothing to say
So he tied him hand and foot and threw him out
Into the night where he will weep no doubt
For this is a warning to those who assume
They can dress how they like
when they meet the groom
You may have accepted Christ's invitation
But whether you're chosen or face damnation
Will be revealed by how you dress
So put on Christ or end up a mess.

The Parable of the Fig Tree

Matt 24:32-44; Mark 13:28-32; Lk 21:29-33

Look at the fig tree and all the trees
When you see their leaves blow in the breeze
Then you know that summer is near.
So God's kingdom is almost here
When you see happen the things I say
And this generation will certainly not pass away
Until all the things I said come about
And I speak the truth without any doubt
Heaven and earth will pass away
But my words remain long past that day.

And indeed what he says has been true
For the words of those men and their deeds too
Continue their influence as they've been heard
They've not passed away,
they remain through the Word.

The Parable of the Ten Virgins

Matt 25:1-13

The kingdom is like ten virgins who went
And took their lamps to a wedding event
Five were foolish and five were wise
The wise took oil perhaps pint-size
The foolish took none they didn't prepare
For the groom took his time before he got there
They all became drowsy and fell asleep.
No sound was heard, no not a peep
Till midnight did come and someone cried out.
"Here's the bridegroom. You must come out!"
The virgins woke up only to find
The wise could see while the foolish were blind
For they used up the oil they needed to see
They had taken the journey much too carefree
They asked the wise to give them some
But the wise told them
where they could buy some from
But while they journeyed to buy the oil
The groom arrived which wasted their toil
For the wise went in and the door was shut closed
The foolish could not enter as they had supposed
They said, "Sir, Open the door for us too!"

Parable Raps

But he replied, "I don't know you."
Therefore keep watch, let the Spirit empower.
For you do not know the day or the hour.

The Parable of the Talents

Matt 25:14-30

A man went away but left his servants some money
"Talents" they're called, though that may seem funny
The master gave to each as he thought best
Not for themselves but for them to invest
To those who have proven to have ability
He gave more money and responsibility
To one he gave five, to another two
And another just one (what did he give you?)
He went on his journey and then he returned
And met with his servants to see what he earned
The one he gave five had made five more
"Good work faithful servant," he said as he swore
To put him in charge of many things
And see what rewards his happiness brings
The man who had two also gain two
"Good! I'll give the same to you"
But the man who was given only but one
When asked what he earned, his profit was none.
But then he began to make an excuse
"You take what you did not produce
So I was afraid and hid in the ground
That talent you gave." He said so profound
The master replied, "You're wicked and lazy.
I'm not stealing from you, are you crazy

Bible Rap

You don't want to work? Then put it in a bank.
You could have earned interest, if I may be so frank
Take the talent from this man and give it to the other
The man who has ten talents and not to his brother
For everyone who has, more will be given
As for this man, he will not be forgiven
Throw him outside where it's dark as night
Let him weep and gnash teeth and have no sight.

The Parable of the Growing Seed

Mark 4:26-29

This is what the kingdom is like
A man scattered seed. Then day and night
Whether he sleeps or wakes the seeds sprout and grow
How does this happen? He doesn't know
All by itself grain is produced
But how that can be he can't deduce.
It grows to a stalk, then head and kernel
All by itself by something internal
As soon as the grain is ripe he reaps
Though much of the work
had been done while he sleeps
So lets not take credit for more than our share
For God does most of the work. That is clear.
But also this means there's not much that you need
God causes growth if you just plant the seed

The Parable of The Watchful Porter

Mk 13:33-37

Be alert! Don't be numb!
For you don't know when the time will come
It's like a man taking a trip
And giving his servants some stewardship
And tells the one at the door
To keep watch. That is his chore.
In evening or midnight, be ready, he warns
Or when the cock crows, when the day dawns
Lest coming suddenly he find you sleeping
Which in the end will lead to you weeping
And this I say to you and to all
Watch! Stay alert! Or else you may fall.

The Parable of The Creditor and the Two Debtors

Lk 7:41-43

A pharisee named Simon had Jesus come over
For dinner to eat perhaps something leftover
Though being a man of much morality
Simon didn't really show much hospitality
But a woman barged in and washed Jesus' feet
While Simon was caught up in his own conceit
For this woman was a sinner maybe even a whore
This woman, Simon thought, Jesus should deplore
But Jesus turned to Simon and told him this story
For Jesus knew his thought and so spoke derogatory

"Two men owed money to a certain lender
One owed 500, he was a big spender
The other owed 50, but neither could pay back
So he canceled the debts, forgiving their lack
Now which of these two
do you suppose would love more"
(Would it be Simon or rather the whore?)
"The one who owed more," Simon replied
Not understanding what Jesus implied.
"You have judged correctly," Jesus said.
"But you did not pour oil on my head,
Nor wash my feet when I came in
But this woman did, this woman of sin.
So I tell you woman, your sins have been forgiven
Before you were dead, but now you're really livin."
So those who love little, may not in Christ abide
But their real problem may just be
that they are filled with pride.

The Parable of the Good Samaritan

Luke 10:30-37

A lawyer once asked,"What must I do
To inherit eternal life, what say you?"
Jesus replied, "What says the Law?"
"To love God and your neighbor without any flaw."
This said the man and Jesus replied,
"Do this and you will be justified."
"But who is my neighbor in what category?"
He said and so Jesus told him this story
A man was going along the way

Parable Raps

And suddenly found himself in great dismay
He was robbed, beaten and left for dead
While the robbers took what they would and fled
A priest happened to go down the street
And saw the man whom the robbers did beat
But he passed him by on the other side
He could have helped, but he did not provide
A Levite also did the same.
But finally a Samaritan came.
When he saw he took pity on him
As the man's prospects were clearly grim
He bandaged his wounds pouring on wine and oil
Caring for him with much toil
He took him to an inn and then the next day
Paid for his care while he went away
But told the innkeeper, "I will return
And pay you any extra that you earn"
Now which of these three do you suppose
Was a neighbor to the man, which do you propose?
"The one who showed mercy," the lawyer replies
Jesus answered, "Go and do likewise."
So if you think by the Law you will be saved
You'd better be more than just well behaved
You must love in spirit and not only in letter
Though you think you're good, you must be better.

The Parable of The Friend in Need

Luke 11:5-13

Suppose at midnight you go to a friend
Ask of him three loaves of bread to lend

Bible Rap

For you say a friend has come over your house
And you have nothing to eat, not even a mouse
But the one inside says, "Don't bother me.
The door is locked and I can't find my key.
I can't get up, we're all in bed
I'm not going to give you any bread."
But as he continued to plead more and more
I tell you the man will open the door.
Not because he was his friend
But just to make his pleading end
So I say: Ask and it will be given to you
And if you seek, you'll find what is true
Knock and you'll suddenly find you're inside
Just as the man did because he had tried
Which of you fathers, if your son has a wish,
Will give him a snake if he asks for a fish?
Or give him a scorpion if he asks for an egg?
Is that what you'd give if your son did beg?
If you then, being evil, know how to give
Good gifts to your children to help them live
How much more will God make it his task
To give his Spirit to those who ask!

The Parable of The Rich Fool

Luke 12:16-21

A rich man's field produced a big gain
But what would he do with all that grain?
"I have no place to store my crops."
I filled my barns all the way to their tops.
I'll tear them down and build ones bigger

Parable Raps

And then retire while I still have vigor
I'll take life easy and bask by the pool
But God said to him, "You are a fool!
Tonight you'll die, you'll go on the shelf
Then who will get
what you prepared for yourself?"
So it will be for those who hoard
Things for themselves but not for the Lord

The Parable of The Faithful and Wise Servant

Luke 12:35-40

Be dressed and ready all the time,
keep your lamps burning
Like men waiting for their master
from the feast returning
So that when he comes you will open up the door
It will be good for such servants, yes forevermore.
For them the master will dress himself to serve
And will treat them kindly just as they deserve
When the master comes, in those servants he'll delight
Though he may have come in the middle of the night.
If you own a house and know when a thief will come
You'd surely be prepared or else you would be dumb.
You also must be ready. Yes, even all the time.
Or the Son of Man may come
just when you commit a crime

The Parable of The Faithful and Wicked Servants

Matt 24:45-51; Lk 12:42-48

It will be good for that servant
whom the Lord puts in charge
Of his fellow servants. His reward will be large
If he carries out his duties a reward he will earn
When the master finds him doing so after his return
He will give him charge of all his possessions.
But concerning his return,
suppose the servant questions
"My master is taking a long time to come,"
And beats some servants and abuses them
He becomes legalistic or perhaps even lawless
His performance is to say the least far from flawless
The master of that servant
will come when he does not expect
Even though that servant
may think he's one of the elect
He'll be cut in pieces and assigned a place
With the unbelievers, rather than in God's grace
If he does not act, though the master's will he knows
He will then be beaten and that with many blows.
But those who do not know, though behaving bad
Will be beaten less than his fellow comrade
From those given much, much will be demanded
So act responsibly or else be reprimanded

The Parable of The Barren Fig Tree

Lk 13:6-9

A man had a fig tree planted in his yard
And could find no fruit though he looked very hard
So he said to the man who took care of the tree
"I've been coming here for how many years? Three!
I've found no fruit in spite of the toil.
Why should it even use up the soil?"
"Sir," he replied, "Leave it one more year,
I'll dig around it and fertilize with care.
If then it bears fruit, that will be good!
If not, we'll make it into firewood."

The Parable of The Lowest Seat

Luke 14:7-11

When someone invites you to a wedding feast
Don't take the best seat, but rather the least
For there may be one more honored than you
Then what do you suppose the host will do?
He'll ask you to give your seat to him
Then your prospects will be rather grim
For you'll have to move to the lowest seat
That's what you'll get for your conceit
But rather you should at first take the lowest place
When the host comes he will then save your face
He will move you to a place which is best
And you will be honored before all the guests
Everyone who exalts himself will be abased

Bible Rap

But those who humble themselves will be raised.

The Parable of Building a Tower and Making War

Luke 14:25-35

To those who followed him did Jesus indicate
If any come to me but really does not hate
His parents and his children and even his own wife
His brothers and his sisters and even his own life
Is not qualified to follow me
This is a cross he must carry
Suppose you want to build a nice tall tower.
Wouldn't you sit down perhaps for an hour
And estimate how much it would cost to build?
For it won't get built just because you willed.
You'll be ridiculed if you can't complete it.
Then you'll feel completely defeated.
Or suppose a king goes out to war.
He has some men, but the other has more.
Will he not consider whether he can win.
He certainly would before the battle did begin.
If he cannot, he'll send a delegation.
And ask for terms of peace from that other nation.
So the cost to follow me is everything you've got
To follow in the way I go, there is no short-cut.
It is good to follow me, just as salt is good
But if you fall away, you've not understood
Salt can't be restored when it's lost its taste
It just cannot be used, but is thrown out as waste

The Parable of The Lost Coin

Luke 15:8-10

Suppose a woman has ten coins and then loses one
Wouldn't she look for it as if it were her son?
And when she does find it, she calls all her friends
So do angels rejoice over one sinner who repents

The Parable of The Lost Son

Luke 15:11-32

A man had two sons and the younger one
Wanted just to have some fun
So he asked his father to give him his share
Of his estate as it seemed fair.
Then he went away and spent all he had
On wild living being really bad
But suddenly a famine came on the land
For which he wasn't prepared beforehand
He got a job feeding swine
And though he was used to drinking wine
He wanted to eat along with the pigs
But he got nothing, no wheat or figs
Then he finally came to his senses
After he considered his consequences
"My father's workers have food to spare,
I'm starving to death while I'm working here.
I'll go back to my father and say this too:
I've sinned against heaven and against you.
I'm not worthy to be called your son

Bible Rap

For I lost that right just to have some fun.
Make me like one of your hired men."
Then he got up and went home again.
But while he was still a long way away
His father saw him, the son gone astray
He was filled with compassion and ran to meet him
He'd been watching and waiting
for the whole interim.
He gave him a hug and then he kissed him
It was quite apparent that he had missed him
The son said, "I have sinned
against heaven and against you.
I can't be your son after what you've been through."
But the father said, "Bring the robe, the one that's best
For this is my son and not just some guest.
Put a ring on his hand and sandals on his feet.
Killed the fattened calf and lets eat some meat.
Let's celebrate and have a feast
For my son is alive after being deceased.
Before he was lost, but now he is found.
Let's celebrate and let joy abound.
The older son was in the field.
Laboring hard so that wheat it would yield
But when he happened to pass by the house
Where all had been quiet as a mouse
He heard music and dancing and asked,
"What's going on?"
"Your brother's returned after he's been long gone."
Said the servants to him of the one who took half,
"And your father has killed the fattened calf."
The brother was angry and refused to go in.
So the father went out to plead with him.

But he answered his father, "I've been slaving for you
All of these years I do what you say I should do.
You never even gave me a goat to eat
With my friends for just a treat.
But when this son of yours has come
Who is really nothing but a bum
He's wasted what's yours on paying for whores
While I do nothing but carry out chores
Yet when he comes you receive him with glee"
"My son," the father said, "you are always with me,
All I have is yours, don't be mad.
But we had to celebrate and be glad.
This brother of yours once was dead
He didn't behave as he was bred
But now he lives, having returned
He was lost and is found and now he has learned
Of my love for him despite his behavior
I'll not condemn, but be his savior.

The Parable of The Shrewd Manager

Luke 16:1-13

There was a rich man whose manager did waste
Much of his things, so he called him in haste
"What is this I hear about you?
Get ready to leave because you are through."
The manager thought, "What shall I do now?
I'm ashamed to beg and I can't even plow.
I know what I'll do so that when I leave
I'll be welcomed elsewhere
and I won't have to grieve."

Bible Rap

So he called each one of his master's debtors
And promised each one to make their debt better
To those owing eight hundred he cut in half
No doubt this would surely make them laugh
From a thousand he wrote
eight hundred bushels of wheat
While the rest of their debt he did delete.
The master commended him for being so shrewd.
So what is my point, to what do I allude?
The world is more shrewd in dealing with its kind
Than are the people of the light.
At least that's what I find.
Use your wealth to gain friends
so that when you pass away
You'll be welcomed into dwellings
forevermore to stay.

Whoever can be trusted with just a little bit
With much he can be trusted as he's shown he's fit
Whoever is unjust with little is unjust with much
So if you've not been faithful
in handling wealth and such
Who will trust you with the riches
which are really true?
So you must be reliable in everything you do
If you have not been faithful with someone's property
You may be given nothing and end in poverty.
No one who's a servant can serve under more than one
Or else he'll end up loving one
and the other loving none.
One he will despise, to other be a sonny.
You cannot both serve God and also serve Money.

The Parable of The Rich Man & Lazarus

Luke 16:19-31

There was rich man dressed in fine linen
Living in luxury though he was sinnin
At his gate lay a beggar, Lazarus by name
Covered with sores being treated with shame
He wanted to eat crumbs from the rich man's table.
Even dogs licked his sore, for he was not able.
Then the time came when the beggar died
And angels carried him to Abraham's side.
The rich man died also his body but a shell
For he awoke to his torment, ending up in hell
He looked up and saw Abraham far away
And Lazarus by his side. That's what he saw that day
He called "Father Abraham have pity on me
And send Lazarus to attend to my plea
For I ask just a bit of water to acquire
For my tongue burns in agony in this fire
But Abraham replied, "Remember my son
You received your good things and had plenty of fun.
While Lazarus had only asked for a crumb
While he suffered he was treated just like a bum
But now he is in comfort and you in agony
That seems rather fair, wouldn't you agree?
And besides all this a big gap has been fixed
Between here and you so we cannot be mixed."
The rich man answered, "Then I beg you
Send him to my house to tell my brothers what's true
So they won't come to this place" (He supposes)
Abraham replied, "They have the prophets and Moses

Let them listen to what is read"
"No," He replied, "Let someone come from the dead.
Then they will listen and even repent."
But he got this reply to his argument
"If they don't listen as the Bible advises
Nor will they listen even though someone rises."

The Parable of The Unworthy Servants

Luke 17:7-10

Suppose you had a slave working all day
And when he comes in, is this what you'd say,
"Come along now and sit down to eat?"
Would he rather not say, "Prepare me some meat,
Get yourself ready and wait on me
For you're my slave and not my employee.
After I've had enough to eat and drink
You can eat too and wash the dishes in the sink"
Would he thank the servant
cause he did what he was told?
He certainly would not. (At least in days of old)
So when you've finished working,
make this declaration:
"We are unworthy servants;
we've only done our obligation."

Parable Raps

The Parable of The Persistent Widow

Luke 18:1-8

Jesus told his disciples a parable one day
That they should not give up when they pray
There once was a judge who really didn't care
Neither for men nor did God he fear
A widow kept coming to him with her plea
"Grant me justice against my adversary."
For some time he refused to hear
But thought, "Though I don't fear God nor do I care,
Yet because this widow keeps bothering me,
It's probably best that I answer her plea,
Else she'll end up wearing me out"
This is what the judge would say, no doubt.
Won't God bring justice for his chosen ones,
Who cry night and day for they are his sons?
Will he keep putting them off?
Certainly not, nor would he scoff.
But when Christ returns will he find on the earth
Such faith so characteristic of the new-birth?

The Parable of the Pharisee and the Tax Collector

Luke 18:9-14

There are some who place confidence in themselves
While looking down on everyone else
To them Jesus told this parable
But if you are proud it may be unbearable.

Bible Rap

Two men went up to the temple to pray
One a tax collector and the other a Pharisee.
The Pharisee prayed to himself in this way
As he stood proudly in the temple that day
"I thank you God that I am not like other men—
robbers, evil doers, adulterers—Amen!
Nor am I like this tax collector the freak.
I give my tithe and fast twice a week.

But the tax collector stood a distance away.
He would not look up to heaven to pray
But beat his breast saying in humility
"God, I'm a sinner have mercy on me."

I tell you that this man, rather than the other
Went home justified, and not his brother
For everyone who exalts himself will be humbled,
For their pride causes them to stumble
And he who is humble will be raised
The proud put down and the humble praised.

Isaiah 53 Rap

The Suffering Messiah

♛

1. Who has believed our message, and to whom has the Lord been revealed?
   He seemed such a common man, to whom has he appealed?
2. And what did attract us to him, no beauty or majesty
   Nothing in his appearance, that people wanted to see.
3. A man of sorrows and suffering, men did reject and also debase
   He was despise and not esteemed, like a man from whom one hid his face
4. Surely he took up our sorrows, yet we reckoned

Bible Rap

him stricken by God
Smitten by him and afflicted, our hearts were oh so hard
5 But he was pierced for our transgressions, and for our sins was broken
But by his wounds we're healed, this is what Isaiah has spoken
6 Like sheep we've gone astray, each turned to his own way
But the iniquity of us all, upon Christ did God lay
7 He was oppressed and also afflicted, yet he submitted to God's will
As a sheep before her shearers, or as lamb that one does kill.
8 By oppression and judgment he was taken away, and left no descendant behind
For he died unmarried and without a child, being stricken in the place of mankind.
9 He died being reckoned as wicked, and buried in a rich man's tomb
Though he had done no violence, nor was deceitful as some did assume
10 Yet it was God's will to crush, and cause him to suffer to death
To make his life a guilt-offering, just as he took his last breath
Yet he lives on and has many children, and through him God's will does thrive
11 For he came back to life again, and many sinners he does justify
12 So he has earned a great portion, because he poured out his life that day.

For he bore the sin of many, and on our behalf he did pray.

John 17 Rap

A Prayer of Jesus

1 Father my time on earth is through
  Glorify me to glorify you
2 You gave me the right to give life eternal
  That I may save people from what is infernal
3 That they may know you, that is your intent and
  Christ Jesus your Son, whom you have sent
4 While on the earth, I brought you glory
  You gave me the work, and I finished the story
5 And now may I glory, when I come home
  As I had long ago, before creatures did roam
6 I've revealed your name, to those you gave me
  And they have obeyed, what you do decree
7 Now they do know, that all comes from you

Bible Rap

Whatever I say, and whatever I do
8 They accepted my word, as holy and pure
They believed you sent me. Of this they were sure
9 Not for the world, but for these I have prayed
For those you have given. For those who have stayed
10 Yours are mine, and mine are for thee
And through them, glory's come to me.
11 I'm coming home, but they remain here
By the power of your name, protect them with care
12 I kept them safe, and gave them instruction
None has been lost, but him doomed to destruction
13 I'm coming to you, but these things I say
So they may have joy, free from dismay
14 Though given your word, yet they are despised
For they're not from the world, just as I am likewise
15 My prayer is not to take them, from this world of sin
But that you protect them, from the devil and his kin
16 They are not of the world, of this I've testified
17 By your word of truth, may they be sanctified
18 As you have sent me, them I've also sent
19 And sanctified myself, to save them from torment
20 My prayer is not for them alone, but also for those others
Who believe their message, those I call my brothers
21 May they be all one, just as you and me

A Prayer of Jesus

That they may be in us, so that the world may see
22 To them I gave the glory, that to me you also gave
So may they be one as us, may it be how they behave.
23 I in them and you in me.
May they be brought to unity.
So that the world may perceive
That you loved them as you loved me.
24 I want those you've given me, to be with me where I am.
To see the glory you've given me, before I was the lamb.
25 Though the world's a stranger, yet I know you well.
And these know you sent me, to save the world from hell.
26 I have made you known to them, and continue to do so.
That your love and me myself, may be in them also.

Apologetics Rap

PERSON 1
Now some people say, "God doesn't exist."
I don't know how such rumors persist.
They say, "We're only a product of chance."
I wouldn't be quick to take that stance
Cause if God is unreal we're nothing but dust
no basis for saying what's just and unjust
no basis for meaning and purpose in life
no basis for love, no basis for strife
The existence of God is really a must
cause people don't really act like dust

PERSON 2A
Some people say, "If God is so real,
why do I suffer so much,
why isn't my life ideal?"

Bible Rap

PERSON 2B
The problem's not with God,
the problem's with you.
Give your life back to God,
and He'll give life back to you.

PERSON 3
Now some people ask,
"How can I know God has spoken?"
Just read His word and I'm not jokin.
Raising the dead and healing the blind.
Oh, there's lots of proofs, you'll find.
In the presence of thousands, both friend and foe.
things not done in secret, don't you know.
For when God speaks His word, He understands
we need proof it's His and not man's.

PERSON 4A
Now some people say, "No peace can I find
no peace in the world, no peace in my mind."

PERSON 4B
Make peace with God and soon you will see
you have peace in your heart and a new destiny.

PERSON 5A
"But maybe all we need for the world to be nice,
is for people to be good. Take my advice"

PERSON 5B
But can you put a band-aid on cancer?
Ethics is nice, but its' no answer.

Apologetics Rap

The problem with people is we're born in sin
but Jesus said you must be born again.
For God so loved the world that He
gave his Son (for you and me).
Those that believe will never die.
but live forever that's no lie.
Freely forgiven, God paid the price,
to wipe out our sins. Now isn't that nice!

PERSON 6A
"But wait, I'm not as bad as you say.
I don't kill people, and I'm not gay."

PERSON 6B
If you think you're good and think you're right
why not turn to God and look at the light?

Song of Redemption

Praise the Father, Praise the Son,
and the Spirit three in one
They alone are God
and through Him all things are

Man in His image He did make
He did this for His own name sake

To bring glory to Him
But the light began to grow dim

> Lord, your glory is above the skies
> May all praises go to you.
>
> Lord, your glory is above the skies
> May all praises go to you

Man he turned away from God

Bible Rap

So his life became so hard
Full of selfishness
His life so meaningless.

Separation from the Lord
God's righteousness could not afford
To just let sin go
So man became his foe.

> Lord, your judgments are right and true.
> All judgment is reserved for you.
>
> Lord, your judgments are right and true.
> All judgment is reserved for you.

But God's love was great for man
So he made Himself a plan
To forgive man's sin
So that life he may enter in.

The Son of God He sent to die
For His wrath to satisfy
It was the only way
The wrath of God to pay

> Lord, your love for us is wide and deep.
> You take our sin and give us life.
>
> Lord, your love for us is wide and deep.
> You take our sin and give us life.

Praise to Jesus God's own Son

Song of Redemption

The victory through Him is won
Down He came to earth
To give us a second birth

Whosoever in Him believes
Eternal life he does receive
The Son of God he'll know
So into heaven he'll go.

> Lord, your glory is above the skies.
> Lord, your judgments are right and true.
> Lord, your love for us is wide and deep.
> Lord, we want to know you.

1 John Rap

1 John 1

1:1 That which was from the start, which we have surely heard
 We saw and touched, and now proclaim, to you that very Word
 2 The life appeared we've seen it, and testify to you
 He once was with the Father, but then became a Jew
 3 We tell you what we saw and heard, have fellowship with us.
 As also with the Father, and with his Son, Jesus. With the Father and his Son, our fellowship is sweet.
 4 We write this message to you, to make our joy complete
 5 And now this is the message, which we've heard from him
 God is light, not dark at all, not even slightly dim.
 6 If we claim to know him, yet in the darkness walk

Bible Rap

We do not live, by the truth, but are lying in our talk
7 If we walk in light, as he is in the light
We'll walk with one another, in fellowship delight
And the blood of Jesus, his one and only Son,
Will also purify our sins, yes each and every one.
8 If we claim to be, without any sinfulness
We do ourselves deceive, and truth is not in us.
9 If we do confess our sins, he's faithful and just too
And will forgive our sins, and make us all brand-new
10 If we claim we have not sinned, we make him out a liar
His word is not in us, we're headed for the fire.

1 John 2

2:1 I write to you my children, so that you will not sin
We have a lawyer on our side, with just the right sheepskin.
Jesus is the Righteous One, who speaks in our defense
He covers all our sin, regardless the offense
2 He's the sacrifice atoning, not only just for us
But also for the whole world, when they believe Jesus.
3 We know we've come to know him, if we do what he says
4 The man who says "I know him," does not Christ possess

1 John Rap

Unless to his commands, he also does comply
Else his claim of knowing him, is nothing but a lie.
5 But if one obeys his word, (such faith is really concrete) in him God's love shows its affect, and is thus made complete.
This is how we know our faith, is not merely talk,
6 Whoever claims to live in him, must just as Jesus walk.
7 The command of which I write, is not new but old,
Even from the beginning, of this you were told.
8 Yet the truth of this command, seems really new
As the darkness is passing away, and light shining through you.
9 Those who claim, to be in the light
But hates his brother, is walking at night
10 Whoever loves his brother, dwells in the light humble,
And there is nothing is him, which would make him stumble
11 Whoever hates his brother, is walking in the dark;
He knows not where he's going, not seeing Christ's footmark
12 I write to you my children, cause your sins have been forgiven
13 You fathers also know him, who was from the beginnen.
I write to you young men, cause you've overcome
The evil one the devil, and have come to know the Son.
You children also I must say, have come to know the Father
14 And I say this once again, if it's not a bother

Bible Rap

He who from the start, you fathers have come to know.
Young men God's word dwells in you, you're above the status quo
You are also strong in Christ, that is what you've become
Not hurt by the devil, but rather him you've overcome

15 Love not the world, nor the things that are therein
If any love the world, God's love is not in him.

16 For all that's in the world, the lust of the eyes
The passions of the flesh, and the pride some do prize
Are not from the Father, but from the world come.
And if you disagree, then you're just being dumb.

17 The world and its desires, will pass away some day
But those who do the will of God, will forever stay.

18 It is the time of the end, and the anti-Christ will come
But even now many do, of whom you've overcome.

19 Consider those who went out from us, they were not of us
For if they were they would remain, but were revealed thus

20 But you are anointed from the Holy One, and the truth all of you know

21 I don't write cause you don't know, but to apply

1 John Rap

it to your foe.

22 The man who denies Jesus as Christ, such a man is a liar
Anti-Christs deny the Father and the Son, and are headed for the fire

23 No one who denies the Son, has the Father. True!
Whoever does acknowledge, the Son has the Father too

24 Let that dwell in you, what you've heard from the start
If it does you'll abide with God, if you keep it in your heart.

25 And this is what he promised us,—even life eternal

26 But I write of those who try and lead you, to a place infernal

27 But the anointing you received from him, continues to dwell in you
It teaches you to discerned, between the false and true.
And just as it has taught you and, continues as your guide
So you shall continue to walk, and in him to abide.

28 And now continue to dwell, in him so that when he appears
You'll be unashamed when he comes, free from any fears

29 If you know that he is righteous, you know that this is true
You know that all who do what's right have been born of him too.

1 John 3

3:1 Behold what manner of love the Father has bestowed on us
That we should be called sons of God having been make righteous.
The reason the world doesn't know us, is because it knew not God.
For Jesus was a stranger to them, so how they treat us is really not odd.
2 We are children of God, and what we will be has not been revealed.
But we know when he appears, we'll be like him as we see him for real.
3 Everyone who has this hope in him, strives to live holy and pure.
For we know we're destined to be like him, and he is holy for sure.
4 Everyone who sins breaks the law, in fact sin is lawlessness
5 But you know when he appears, he'll give us perfect flawlessness.
6 No one who keeps on sinning. No one who continues to sin
Has seen or know Christ our Lord, nor does Christ live in him.
7 And this I say to you dear children, let no one lead you astray
He who does what is right is righteous, just as Christ is righteous (I'll say!)
8 Those who are of the devil, practice a lifestyle of sinning

1 John Rap

For the devil also has been sinning, and that from the beginning

9 Of those who live a lifestyle of sin, not one is born of God.
God's seed dwells in them changing their life, so from such a life they are barred.

10 Because of this fact we can know, who God's children are
And also identify those of the devil, for their behavior is like a scar.
For those who don't do what is right, are not children of God but another.
And the same goes for him, who does not love his brother.

11 This is the message you've heard from the start: we should love everyone who believes

12 Don't be like Cain who killed his brother, who belonged to the one who deceives
Cain killed him cause his works were evil, but his brother's were righteous and good

13 Don't be surprise my brothers, if you're hated for doing what you should

14 Thus we can know from this also, that we have passed from death to life
Because we do love our brothers. Those who don't remain under the knife.

15 A murderer is anyone who hates, his brother and his prospects are grim
For you know that no murderer, has eternal life in him.

16 This is how we know what love is: Christ Jesus laid his life down

So we should do the same, for our brothers in view of the crown.
17 He who sees his brother in need, and has stuff but not any pity
How can the love of God be in him, he's not on the way to God's city.
18 Let us not love with words or tongue, but in action and in truth.
19 By this we know we belong to God, when we see him our hearts he'll sooth
20 Whenever our hearts condemn us, let's remember how we've behaved
For if we have loved our brothers, that indicates we've been saved.
21 And if our hearts don't condemn us, then we can be bold before God
22 and receive from him what we ask, because all his commands we regard.
23 And what's his command you may ask, but to believe in the name of his Son
And also to love one another, that's what he commands everyone.
24 Those who obey his commands, do with him abide.
But how do we know he lives in us? By the Spirit he gave as a guide.

1.John 4

4:1 Do not believe everyone that you hear, but test the spirits to see
If they're from God, or not in which case, feel

1 John Rap

free to disagree.
For many false prophets have gone through the world, of this you can be sure
Compare what you hear with the Bible, to discern the corrupt and pure.

2 Some teach Christ came in spirit, but not in physical flesh.
3 Such teachers are not from God, and don't with the truth mesh.
Anti-Christ is this kind of spirit, which you heard is coming in the end
But even now already, it's in the world ready to contend.
4 You dear children are from God, and have overcome such a spirit.
Because the one in you is greater, than the one in the world (I swear it!)
5 They are from the world, and speak from its perspective.
The world listens to them, so no surprise, that their speech is rather effective.
6 But we are from God so remember, whoever listens to us knows God.
But those who don't listen, to what we say, knows not him nor should you regard.
7 Dear friends let us love one another, for from God does come love
And I say everyone who loves, knows God and is born from above.
8 Whoever does not practice love, does not so much as know God
Because God does encompass, all that is love, so

Bible Rap

---

this should not seem very odd.
9 This is how God showed his love, he sent down his one true Son
Into the world, so that we might live, together through him as one
10 It wasn't because we loved God, that he sent his Son to atone
But because God love us, and so made such a fuss, to pay for our sins alone.
11 Dear friends since God so love us, we also should love one another
This is how we respond, to the way God love us, by each one loving his brother.
12 No one has even seen God, if we love God lives in us
God reveals through us, his love made complete, having also made us righteous.
13 We know that we live in him, and in us he also lives
Cause he's given us of his Spirit, and all of our sins he forgives.
14 We have seen and do testify, the Father has sent a Savior
Into the world, the Son of his love, which also affects our behavior.
15 If anyone does acknowledge, Christ Jesus the Son of God.
God lives in him, and he in God, and this you should not find odd.
16 And so we know and rely, on the love that God has shown
God is love, and those who live, in love are truly

1 John Rap

God's own
17 Thus love is made complete among us, so we will not fear
The judgment of God, cause in this world, we like Christ appear.
18 There is no fear in love, God's love for us drives it away
The one who has fear, is not perfect in love, and may not be prepared for that day
19 We love cause he first loved us, we were not the ones to start
Our love for other Christians, is because we took God's love to heart.
20 If anyone says, "I love God," but hates his brother has lied
For his brother he sees, and God he cannot, so by his works what he says is denied.
21 And this is the command he gives us, that whoever does say he loves God
Must also love his brother, and this I don't think is too hard.

5:1 Everyone who believes, Jesus is Christ, has been born from above
All who love their father, his child they also love.
2 We know we love God's children, and this is how we know
We know by loving God, as keeping his commands do show.
3 For this is love for God, to obey his commands
And his commands are not a burden, for he who truly understands

Bible Rap

4 For all who've been born of God, overcome this world of sin by this faith, we have this victory, and it is Christ our faith is in.

5 And let met ask this one more time, who is it that has overcome?
But he who believes in the Son of God, yes through Jesus he has won.

6 Jesus Christ came, by water and blood, and not by water alone.
And the Spirit is one of truth, and this is what he's shown.

7 For three bear witness in heaven, the Father the Word and the Spirit.

8 While on the earth, the Spirit and water and blood, these three do bear it

9 If we accept the witness of men, God testimony is greater.
For this is the witness, God gave of his Son, against Him I won't be a debater

10 He who believes in the Son of God, to this his heart testifies.
Those who don't believe, are saying that God lies.

11 And this is the testimony, God gave us life eternal.
And where is this life? But in the Son, given to us internal.

12 He who possesses the Son, has this life forever.
He who has not the Son, has not this life, no never.

13 I write unto you who believe, on God's Son whose name is Jesus.
So that you may know as a fact, and telling you this does please us
That eternal life you possess, if indeed you do

1 John Rap

believe
And if you don't, so that you may believe, and also the Son receive.

5:14 And this is the boldness, that we have in him.
If we ask anything he hears us, if we ask from his will not a whim.

15 And if we know that he hears us, whatever it is we may ask
We know that we have what we asked from him, let us set out for our task

16 If anyone sees his brother, commit a sin not unto death
Let's ask God, to give him the life, and to take him out from the depth.
There is a sin unto death, for it prayer is ineffective

17 There's sin not to death, though all sin is wrong, this is the right perspective

18 Everyone born of God, lives not a lifestyle of sin
But keeps himself from the devil, who cannot harm him within.

19 We know we are children of God, and the world lies under the devil

20 We know God's Son has come, (and I'm speaking on the level)
To give us an understanding, that we may know him who is true.
He's the true God life eternal, and his Son Christ lives in you.

21 Therefore I tell you beware, of false imitations by men.
For God is defined in the Bible, reject all idols.
Amen

James Rap

James 1

A Christian should be joyful if he finds
He faces many trials of different kinds.
Endure through trials, they'll make you new.
Endurance itself will become a part of you.
And if, in fact, you do endure
You'll find that you become more mature
And if you don't know what to do.
Just ask God, He'll answer you.
But ask believing without doubt.
For surely God can figure it out.
He who doubts is like a wave of the sea
Blown and tossed by the wind he must be.
Don't think he will receive from the Lord.
Double-minded, unstable, full of discord.
The humble brother ought to take pride
For in a high position he does abide.
The rich should also take pride, you know,
Because his position is really low.

Bible Rap

Like a wild flower that passes away
So he will fade from the scene and his riches decay.
Those who endure through trials and don't fall down
Will in the end receive a crown.
When tempted no one should dare to say,
"God is tempting me," for there is no way.
God cannot be tempted by sin.
Over Him no evil can ever win.
Nor does He cause you to stray.
So you're not really right in what you say.
We're tempted by our own desires.
We're dragged away into the fire.
After desire does conceive,
It gives birth to sin and so we grieve.
And sin when it is full-grown,
Gives birth to death, and so we moan.
My dear brothers, don't be deceived.
Every good gift is from above I perceive.
Coming down from the Father of light
Who doesn't shift from left to right.
He gave us birth through the word of truth,
That we may be a kind of first fruit.
Be slow to speak and quick to hear,
For we have one mouth, but more than one ear.
Be slow to anger, for it never acquires,
The righteous life that God desires.
Moral filth and evil put aside,
And let the word in you abide.
If in meekness this be your goal,
The word will surely save your soul.
Do the word, don't just be a hearer,
Like a man looking into a mirror.

James Rap

He turns away, and yes he does
Forget what kind of man he was.
But if you look into the word with care,
Not forgetting what you hear,
And doing what it says to you,
You'll be blessed in what you do.
If you think you're a religious man,
Control you're tongue, if you can.
Else I could only say,
You're religion isn't worth the time of day.
Religion that's perfect, God confesses,
Is to help orphans and widows in their distresses,
And to keep oneself from being polluted,
For sin in the world is firmly rooted.

James 2

Now if we're brethren in reality,
Then we shouldn't show partiality.
Suppose a man comes into your meeting.
And you welcome him with a friendly greeting,
"You sit here in a good place."
You say with eloquence and grace,
Because with fine apparel he is clothed,
And on his hand, a ring of gold.
Then a poor man comes to you.
And you tell him what to do,
"You stand there, or sit by my feet."
Both men with equality you should treat.
You are judges with evil thoughts,
For though there are people of many sorts,
To treat people different because of money,

Bible Rap

Seems to me to be kind of funny.
For God did choose those who are poor,
To be rich in faith, and there's more,
To inherit the kingdom he promised those
Who love the one that arose.
So why insult the poor, I say
The rich exploit you day by day.
If the royal law you fulfill
"Love you neighbor as yourself," you do well.
But if you treat some greater or lesser
You're convicted by the law as a transgressor.
For if you keep the whole law,
But miss one point, you are guilty of all.
He said don't commit adultery, nor kill.
But if you do only one, you are guilty still.
So speak and act as those who will be
Judged by the law of liberty.
If with mercy we judge sin
Then mercy over judgment will inevitably win.
My dear brothers, what does it gain
If one believes, but only in vain.
For if faith does not affect how he behaves,
I don't really think that kind of faith saves.
If a brother or sister is naked or poor,
And you say "be warmed and filled," but do no more.
Just as they profit nothing from what you said,
Faith without works is really dead.
Some say, "You have faith, I have deeds"
But don't you think where that leads?
Our faith is revealed by what we do
So if you have faith, you'll have deeds too!
You believe there's one God, you do well.

James Rap

Even demons believe and tremble in hell.
But don't you know that even God said
That faith without works is really dead.
Was not Abraham by works justified
When on the mountain by God he was tried.
You see his faith and deeds did meet
And by his deeds, his faith was complete.
And so the scripture was fulfilled in what is says,
"Abraham believed and was
reckoned righteousness."
And he was called the friend of God.
But with the faith he had, that's not really odd.
Faith that works, that's the kind
that justifies a man, I find.
That Rahab the harlot was justified
By what she did, can't be denied.
She received the messengers and let them stay
And sent them out another way.
For as the body without the spirit is dead.
So too if faith and actions are not wed.

James 3

Not many should presume to teach.
God strictly judges what they preach.
We all in many ways stumble.
If you don't think so, you're just not humble.
The tongue is like a small rudder,
Steers ships through the wind, just like butter,
Or like a bit in a horse's mouth,
You can make him turn either north or south.
It seems it has so much control.

Bible Rap

With it we gain and lose our soul.
A forest can burn from a little spark.
So our tongue can make our whole life dark.
All kinds of animals we can tame,
But controlling the tongue is just no game.
But let me tell you something worse,
With it we praise and then we curse.
This is not suppose to be.
Can figs and olives come from the same tree?
You think you're wise and you understand
But maybe you're living in dreamland.
Show me you're works done in humility
Or else you're just talkin vanity.
But if selfish envy fills your heart,
Don't tell it to me nor from the truth depart.
Such wisdom's not from God it's from the devil,
It ends in disorder, it's not on the level.
But the wisdom from above is pure as snow.
It's peace-loving and considerate, don't you know.
Submissive and merciful, full of good fruit,
Impartial, sincere that you can't dispute.
Sow in peace and reap a harvest of right.
Selfish envy will end up without any light.

James 4

From where do fights and quarrels come?
From your desires within, are you so dumb?
You murder and covet and cannot get
You lust and do not have, I'll bet.
I'll tell you what you need to do
Just ask God, He'll answer you.

James Rap

But remember that God will surely measure
Whether you're going to spend it on you pleasure.
Rather ask so as to serve the Lord.
With riches in heaven He will reward.
And don't as much with the world make friends,
Because you know how the story ends.
Don't make God's Spirit jealous.
God opposes the proud, doesn't He tell us.
So if you think you're going to stumble,
Just remember that God gives grace to the humble.
Submit to God, resist the devil.
When he flees from you, in God you'll revel.
Draw near to God and He'll come to you.
Repent from sin and see what God will do.
Grieve and mourn, wail and cry.
Change your laughter to mourn
and to joy say "goodbye"
And if you do drink from this cup,
The Lord Himself will lift you up.
You know your brothers you should not slander
But let me speak with some candor.
He who speaks evil and judges his brother
Also speaks evil and judges another
He judges the law and speaks against it
But when against the law in judgment you sit
And don't bother doing what it says
You'll have one to judge you, I must confess.
There's only one who will save and destroy
But when you judge you're brother
you do Him annoy.
Now listen you who like to say,
I've got plans for my life, I'll have success some day.

But you don't even know tomorrow
which may, in fact, end in sorrow.
For what is your life? It's only a mist.
It will vanish soon, if you catch my gist.
Instead, this is what you ought to say,
"If it's God's will, we will venture this way."
As it is you brag and boast.
Don't be surprised if you end up like toast.
And if you know what is the good to do,
And don't do it. Well that's sin too.

James 5

Now listen you rich, weep and wail.
For as days pass, so your riches fail.
Your wealth has rotted, as I've noted,
Your gold and silver are corroded.
Their corrosion should cause you some concern.
For on judgment day, your flesh will burn.
Be patient my brothers until the Lord come.
As the farmer waits for the land until autumn
To yield its fruit with the spring rains
You too be patient and stand firm through the pains.
For the Lord's coming is really quite near.
So surely you can with each other bear.
Don't grumble against the brothers, not anymore
For the Judge is now standing right at the door.
As an example of faith that stands under trial
Take the prophets who endured for quite a long while.
We count them blessed who have persevered
Despite what they faced and what they feared.

James Rap

Or consider the story of Job and his foes,
Well I'm sure that you know how that story goes.
The Lord is full of compassion and grace
That's why Job wanted to see him face to face.
Above all my brothers, do not swear
By heaven or earth, or by things here or there.
Let your "yes" be yes and your "no," no
Or you'll be condemned by what you sow.
Is anyone of you in trouble today?
Take my advice, just let him pray.
Is anyone happy? Let him sing praise.
Is anyone sick? Here's what God says.
Let him call the elders and pray in one accord.
And anoint him with oil in the name of the Lord.
And the prayer of faith will make him well
The Lord will raise him up from his sick spell
If he has sinned, he will be forgiven.
So confess your sins and let prayer be given.
The prayer of the righteous, from God's perspective,
Is full of power and really effective.
Elijah was a man who like us appeared.
He prayed and it did not rain for over three years.
Again he prayed and then it did rain
And the earth produced both wheat and much grain.
If one of you strays from the truth
Whether he's old or still a youth
And one turns him to the right path
He saves a soul from God's wrath.

1 Peter Rap

1Peter 1

1:1 Peter, an apostle of Jesus Christ
To God's elect scattered like mice.
Throughout Pontus and Cappadocia,
Galatia, Asia, and Bithynia,
  2 Chosen by God as He did foreknow,
Sanctified by the Spirit from your head to your toe.
Who helped you to hear and so to obey
The gospel of Christ, which is really the way
His blood alone did cleanse you from sin
And so Grace and peace he did for you win.
  3 Praise be the God, the Father above
Who gave us new birth because of his love
And now we have hope to be raised from the dead.
Just as Jesus was raised, that's what he said.
  4 Inheriting things that cannot spoil or fade
Kept in heaven for you, the ones who obeyed.

Bible Rap

5 Who by faith are shielded by God's power and might
 Until the Lord comes when the time is just right.
6 In this you really have been overjoyed,
 Despite all the trials you could not avoid.
7 That your faith may be tested like gold in the fire
 Faith that is true has a value much higher
 For from it comes praise and honor and glory
 When Jesus comes back we'll hear the whole story.
8 You love him by faith though him you can't see
 By faith you have joy full of glory.
9 For you are receiving your faith's final goal
 Which is to be saved and to be made whole.
10 Of this salvation the prophets did write
 Asking the Spirit during the day and the night
11 To reveal to them what manner of time
 (Oops! Can't think of a really good rhyme)
 They wanted to know the time and the place
 Christ would suffer and then glory embrace
 What they saw, you now see
12 When they spoke the words of prophecy
 Which you heard from the message of love
 By the Spirit of God sent from heaven above
 Even angels long to look into these
 It seems they can't do so with much ease.
13 Get ready for action, be self-controlled
 and set your hope fully on what was foretold
 of the grace to be given to you from above
 When Jesus returns for the ones he does love
14 As obedient children, do not conform
 to your evil desires when you thought them the

1 Peter Rap

norm
15 But just as holy as he who called you
16 be holy yourselves in all that you do
17 since your father is judge of each man's works
   who impartially judges both the wise and the jerks
   live your lives as strangers here and treat your
   father above with reverent fear
18 For you weren't redeemed by silver or gold not
   by things that perish or even grow old
19 but with the precious blood of Christ, a lamb
   without spot or blemish, not even a gram
20 He himself was chosen too,
   but now revealed for me and you
21 through Him you believe in God who raised
   Christ from the dead as the guards were amazed
   And glorified Him much higher than the pope,
   and so in God are both your faith and your hope
22 Now that you have obeyed the truth and purified
   yourself from the sins of your youth so that your
   love for the Christians is sincere love them
   deeply and with care
23 For you have been born again of seed
   that lasts forever, that's what I read
   for the seed is God's word, which will always
   endure
   it lives and is active and makes you mature
24 For men are like grass, and their glory like flowers
   They can wither and die in just a few hours
25 But God's Word lasts forever, that's really true
   And this was the word that was preached to you.

Bible Rap

1Peter 2

2:1 Get rid of all malice, deceit, hypocrisy
Envy and slander, which may not be easy
2 Like newborns crave milk feed on the word
Grow in your spirit till you've fully matured
3 That is if you've tasted how good the Lord is
Born of His Spirit and become fully His
4 As you come to Him, the living stone
Who was rejected by men, but He was God's own
5 You also who are stones, and not just wood
Are being made into a house, yes a holy priesthood
Offering sacrifices to God through the Lord
Which are pleasing to God and never make him bored
6 See I lay a stone in Zion is what the Scriptures say
The one who trusts in him, will never find dismay.
7 Now precious is this stone to you who do believe what's said
But those who don't, reject the stone that really is the head
8 A stone that causes men to stumble and also to fall down
Who stumbled cause they disobeyed not destined for a crown
9 But you are a chosen people, kings and priests too
To declare the praise of him who to the light brought you

1 Peter Rap

10 Once you were no people, but now God's people you are
   You once received no mercy, now mercy's not so far
   As a fellow stranger in this world of sin
11 Abstain from those desires that harm your soul within.
12 Live good lives among the pagan, though accused of doing wrongs
   That they may see and glorify God one day in praise by singing songs.
13 Submit yourselves for the Lord's sake
   To every authority that man may make
14 To the king as supreme and governors too
   Sent to punish and reward whatever you do.
15 This is the way God wants you to walk
   To silence the foolish and ignorant talk
16 Live as free men without evil intents
   Servants of God, that only makes sense.
17 Show proper respect, to all honor bring
   To Christians, and God and even the king
18 Slaves submit to your masters too
   Whether they're good or bad, in whatever you do
19 For isn't it good if a man bears the pain
   To suffer unjustly and so honor gain
20 But if you suffer for the wrong you may do
   There's no credit God must give, no reward for you
21 Christ also suffered and so you should to
   Follow His path that he set for you
22 He committed no sin nor could you find
   Deceit in his mouth, no not of the kind

23 They insulted Him, but he didn't react
   With vengeance and threats, and that is a fact.
   But entrusted Himself to God who's the judge
   For God's answer to sin was nothing to fudge
24 He bore our sins when He hung on a tree
   So we might die to sins and live righteously
25 By His wounds you are healed, though sheep gone astray
   but now have returned to the Shepherd to stay.

1Peter 3

3:1 Wives should submit though your husbands are not saved
   To win them not by words, but by how you behave
2 When they see how pure you live your life
   And the reverence you have rather than strife.
3 Let not your beauty come from outward things
   Like hair and clothes and wearing rings
4 Your inner self is of greater merit
   If you have a gentle and quiet spirit
5 For this is the way holy women of old
   Gained favor by doing what they were told
6 Like Sarah who obeyed and called her husband master.
   Do right, fearlessly is what she'd say if you asked her.
7 Husbands treat them with respect
   Or else with God you won't connect
8 Be of one mind sympathize with each one
   Loving and humble, just like the Son
9 Repay not with evil those who insult you

1 Peter Rap

But rather with blessing and inherit one too
10 If you want to see good days and live for quite awhile
Keep from speaking evil and your lips from speaking guile
11 Repent and do the good you know you really ought to do
And seek the peace of God that's what you really must pursue
12 The Lord sees and hears the righteous of the land
But when face to face with God, the evil will not stand
3:13 And who will bring the harm to you if you do the good
So you should in everything do the good you should
14 But even if you suffer for doing what is right
How blessed you are and unlike them don't have fear nor fright
15 But in your hearts make Christ the Lord, ready to respond
To everyone who asks you of the hope you have beyond
16 With gentleness and respect keep your conscience clear
So to shame the ones who speak against your good works here.
17 It is better if it really be the will of God
To suffer for the right you do, though it may be hard
18 For Christ did also suffer once the just one in our stead

Bible Rap

Being put to death in flesh, then risen from the dead
19 By that Spirit also preached to those who misbehaved
20 Who disobeyed in Noah's time, when only 8 were saved.
21 The flood of Noah is a type of washing that saves you
Not from dirt but to pledge your conscience to be true
22 Unto God who saves you by the one he gave the crown
The Christ who reigns at God's right hand and all to him bow down

1Peter 4

4:1 Since Christ suffered, have the same mind
For those who cease from sin will suffer as Christ in kind
 2 Do not live your earthly life for your own desire
But rather live to do God's will and set your goals much higher
 3 You spent enough time in the past doing what pagans do
Carousing at drunken orgies and worshipping idols too
 4 They think it strange you do not plunge into the flood as they
 5 They heap abuse, but God will judge them on the last day
 6 For to this end the gospel was preached to those

1 Peter Rap

who are now dead
Though judged by men they live with God, just like the scriptures said
7 The end of all things is near, I say
Watch and be sober so you can pray
8 Love each other deeply, for love covers many a sin
9 Be hospitable without grumbling if someone need to move-in
10 As each one has received let him served one another
So that God may be praised by serving your brother.
11 If anyone speaks, let him speak as God would
If anyone serves, let him do as he should
With all the strength that God supplied
That in all things God may be glorified.
12 Do not be surprised at the trials you go through
As if something strange were happening to you
13 But rejoice that you share in Christ's suffering
That when He does return, oh what joy that will bring
14 If you are insulted for Christ, you are blessed
For upon you does the Spirit of God rest
15 Don't suffer for a crime, with the shame it brings
Or even as a meddler in other people's things
16 Suffer as a Christian and in that there is no shame
But rather you should praise the Lord that you bear that name
17 For judgment starts right now with God's family
18 And if with us the judgment starts, what will the outcome be

Bible Rap

For those who don't obey the gospel of the Lord
If we are scarcely saved, on them will wrath be poured
19 Therefore let them suffering doing as they should
Commit themselves to God and continue doing good.

1Peter 5

5:1 To the elders among you I appeal as a fellow elder too
A witness of Christ's sufferings and who will share in His glory with you
2 Be shepherds of God's flock given to your trust
Serve willingly as God would want and not because you must
Not greedy for the money, but serving eagerly
3 Not lording it over the flock of God, but examples you must be
4 And when the Chief Shepherd comes on judgment day
You will get a crown that will never fade away
5 Let all be submissive with humility rather than grumble
For God opposes the proud but gives grace to the humble
6 Humble yourselves under God's mighty hand
And you will be honored when before Him you stand
7 Cast upon Him all your troubles and cares
For He cares about all your worries and fears
8 Be sober and alert in every hour

1 Peter Rap

    For the devils is watching for one to devour
9 You should resist him, standing firm in your faith
    Knowing your brothers share the same fate
10 And the God of all grace who called you to glory
    After you have suffered a while in his-story
    Will make you strong and restore you again
11 To Him be the power forever. Amen
12 With the help of Silas, who works very hard
    I write to you briefly of the true grace of God
13 The church in Babylon chosen with you
    Sends you greetings as Mark does too
14 Greet one another with a kiss of love
    Peace to all in Christ, below and above.

2 Peter Rap

2Peter 1

2:1 Peter an apostle and servant of Christ
To those who obtained a faith so nice
So precious to us it affects our behavior
By the righteousness of our God and Savior
3 May grace and peace to you abound
As in the knowledge of God it may be found
His power has given all we need
For a godly life, if we heed
To our knowledge of Him who called us by His glory
And His goodness too, just as in the story.
4 Through these He has given promises so great
So that in God's nature you may participate
And escape the corruption the world inspires
Which are caused by evil desires
5 For this very reason try very hard
To add goodness to your faith just like God
6 And to your goodness knowledge also self-

Bible Rap

    control
7 Perseverance and godliness add to your soul
    And be kind as brothers like your Father above
    And last but not least you must add love
8 If these qualities in you grow
    They will make you fruitful from what you know
9 But if one has not one of these kind
    He is nearsighted and even blind
    For wasn't the point to be cleansed from sin?
    And doesn't he now call Jesus kin?
10 Be careful to make sure your call
    For if you do these things you will never fall
11 And you will receive a rich entry
    Into the kingdom (maybe this century!)
12 I will remind you of these things long-term
    Even though you know them and in the truth stand firm
13 I think that it is right to refresh your memory
    As long as I may live in this tent of my body
14 Because I really feel I will soon put it aside
    As Jesus made it clear to me and with him I'll abide
15 I will make every effort to see that when I go
    You will remember all these things I know.
16 I tell you we didn't invent the story
    But saw Jesus himself in his glory
17 For he received honor from the Father who spoke from the sky
    I am quite certain and we don't lie
18 We heard this voice that came from above
    On that mountain he said "This is my Son whom I love"

2 Peter Rap

19 The word of the prophets is made more sure
   Pay attention to it as if it were
   A light that was shining in a dark place
   Until you see Jesus face to face
20 But firstly know that no prophet's oration
   Was a matter of the prophet's own interpretation
21 Prophecy never came from man's will as I hear it
   But men spoke from God as they were carried by the Spirit

2Peter 2

2:1 Now there used to be false prophets among the people too
   Just as there will be false teachers yes even among you
   They teach destructive heresies in secret do they offend
   even denying the Lord who bought them—destruction is their end.
2 To their shameful ways many will follow suite
   And bring the way of truth into disrepute
3 In their greed these teachers exploit you with stories they made up
   Their condemnation awaits them and destruction when they wake up
4 For if God did not spare the angels when they fell
   And put them in dungeons for judgment down in hell
5 And if He didn't spare the ungodly from the flood

Bible Rap

    But protected Noah and seven others from getting covered with mud
6 If He destroyed Sodom and Gomorrah after the angels had their dinner
    And made them an example of what's to become of the sinner
7 And if He rescued righteous Lot distressed all his days
8 By the lives of these lawless men bisexuals and gays
9 If this is so, God can rescue godly men
    And hold the lawless for that day, Praise God, Amen!
10 And especially those who follow their corrupt desires
    And despise authorities they are such liars
11 For they are not afraid to slander dignitaries
    Bold and arrogant they are as if God's emissaries
    Although stronger even angels do not bring
    Such accusations in the presence of the King
12 These men blaspheme in matters they do not understand
    But like beasts they will be taken from the land
13 They will be paid for the harm they have done
    For to them to carouse in the daytime is fun
    They are blots and blemishes reveling in their pleasure
    As they feast with you at their own leisure
14 With eyes full of adultery they never stop sinning
    They seduce the unstable and in greed they always try winning
15 They left the way and followed after Baal

2 Peter Rap

Who loved the wages of sin along the trail
16 But was rebuked for doing wrong by a mule
Who spoke with a man's voice and restrained the fool
17 These men are springs without water and mists driven by storms
Black darkness is reserved for them in hell where it's quite warm!
18 For they mouth empty boastful words by appealing to the flesh
Enticing those just escaping a life in which sin they mesh
19 They promise them freedom, while they are but slaves
For a man is not free if to his flesh he obeys
20 If from such corruption they find their way free
By the knowledge of the Lord, yet they don't flee
But are once again entangled and are overcome
They're worst of at the end than where they started from
21 It may have been better for them not to have known the way of truth
Than to have turned their backs on the sacred command which they knew even in their youth
22 Of them the proverb is true "To its vomit returns the dog"
So also to them it is true "to the mud returns the clean hog."

2Peter 3

3:1 This is my second letter to you

Bible Rap

2 To remind you to think on things you once knew
  Recall the words spoken by the prophets of old
  And the command of Christ through the apostles being told
3 First of all you must understand
  That scoffers will come and take their stand
4 They will say "Where is this coming foretold
  For everything is as it was of old"
5 But they forget that long ago
  God's word made the heavens and the earth below
  The earth was formed from water—that's right—H2O
6 By which the ancient world was destroyed as you know
7 By the same word they are reserved for fire
  As also are the mocker, the sinner and liar
8 But do not forget this one thing I say
9 With the Lord a thousand years is as a day
  Concerning His promise the Lord is not slow
  But patient with you lest to hell you might go
10 The Lord will come in the night like a thief
  And destroy everything, that is my belief
11 What kind of people should you then ought you to be
  You ought to live right and also holy
12 As you look forward to the day of the Lord
  Though it brings death, yet that you can afford
13 For also it will bring a new heaven and earth
  That is for those who have gone through the new birth
14 So then dear friends during this interim

2 Peter Rap

Be found spotless and blameless and at peace with him
15 Keep in mind that God's patience means salvation
Just as Paul wrote with God's inspiration
16 He writes the same way in all his letters
Speaking in them of all these matters.
Though some things he says are hard to understand
Which some do distort, them I must reprimand
For they do so to other scriptures as well
But in the end they may end up in hell
17 Therefore dear friends, be on your guard
Lest you be carried away and you fall really hard
18 But grow in the grace and knowledge of our Savior
To Him be the glory now and forevermore.

Becoming a Christian

Becoming a Christian involves entering the Kingdom of God. To enter the kingdom we must acknowledge and submit to the King.

> *"if you will confess with your mouth the Lord Jesus, and believe in your heart that God raised him from the dead, you will be saved. For with the heart, one believes unto righteousness; and with the mouth confession is made unto salvation."*
> **Romans 10:9,10**

The Message of Salvation
What God Did

God created people to have a relationship with Himself. We were made in the image of God, but *"for all have sinned, and fall short of the glory of*

Bible Rap

God." **Romans 3:23** Man is sinful but God is holy and so there is a separation between the two. *"Behold, Yahweh's hand is not shortened, that it can't save; neither his ear heavy, that it can't hear: but your iniquities have separated between you and your God, and your sins have hidden his face from you, so that he will not hear."* **Isaiah 59:1,2**

This separation ends in judgment and death, both physical and eternal.

> *"For the wages of sin is death."* **Romans 6:23a**

> *"But for the cowardly, unbelieving, sinners, abominable, murderers, sexually immoral, sorcerers, idolaters, and all liars, their part is in the lake that burns with fire and sulfur, which is the second death."* **Revelation 21:8**

There are various ways in which people have tried to bridge the gap to return to God, but all fall short.

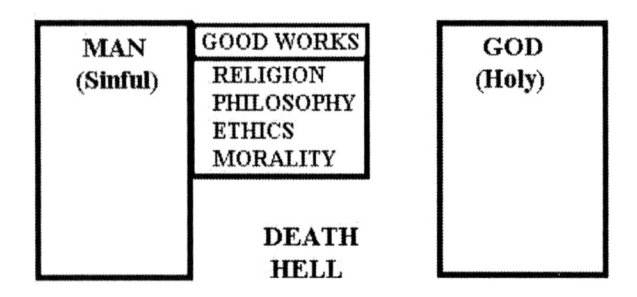

MAN (Sinful)	GOOD WORKS / RELIGION / PHILOSOPHY / ETHICS / MORALITY	GOD (Holy)
	DEATH HELL	

Becoming a Christian

"Because by the works of the law, no flesh will be justified in his sight. For through the law comes the knowledge of sin. But now apart from the law, a righteousness of God has been revealed, being testified by the law and the prophets; even the righteousness of God through faith in Jesus Christ to all and on all those who believe. For there is no distinction, for all have sinned, and fall short of the glory of God; being justified freely by his grace through the redemption that is in Christ Jesus." **Romans 3:20-24**

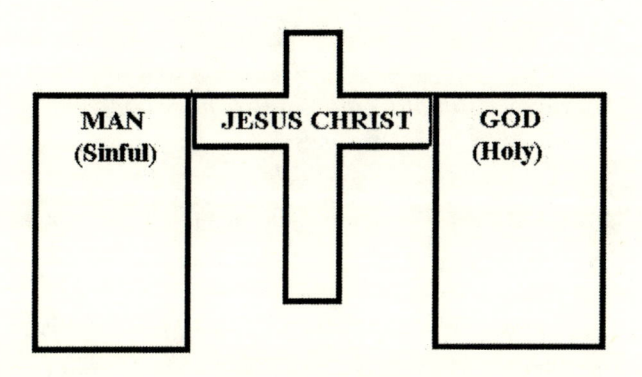

| MAN (Sinful) | JESUS CHRIST | GOD (Holy) |

"For God so loved the world, that he gave his one and only Son, that whoever believes in him should not perish, but have eternal life." **John 3:16**

By dying on the cross, Jesus Christ satisfied the demands of God's justice that sin be paid for. So you can either pay for your own sins in hell, or you can accept Christ's substitutionary atonement as payment to God on your behalf. For through Christ God now offers your sins to be freely and graciously forgiven. This is not earned, but accepted by faith.

> *"Now to him who works, the reward is not counted as grace, but as debt. But to him who doesn't work, but believes in him who justifies the ungodly, his faith is accounted for righteousness."* **Romans 4:4,5**

Having believed, God makes us into new creatures.

> *"Therefore if anyone is in Christ, he is a new creation. The old things have passed away. Behold, all things have become new."* **2Corinthians 5:17**

This is the New Covenant God has made with believers:

> *"This is the covenant that I will make with them: 'After those days,' says the Lord, 'I will put my laws on their heart, I will also write them on their mind;' then he says, 'I will remember their sins and their iniquities no more.'"* **Hebrews 10:16,17**

The truth of the gospel message was affirmed by Christ's fulfillment of Old Testament prophecies and by his miracles and in particular by his resurrection from the dead.

Becoming a Christian

Qualifying for Salvation
What You Need To Go Through

God has a treasure, it's hidden away
But seek and you shall find some day
That treasure he offers which is life through the Son
A life which will last after your life here is done

There are those who seek from place to place
What can be found only through God's grace
The pearl of great price is Jesus our Lord
When you find Him you'll find that you can afford
To replace your trust in other things
With the One from whom eternal life springs

The salvation that God offers is spoken of as being a gift. *"For the wages of sin is death, but the free gift of God is eternal life in Christ Jesus our Lord."* **Romans 6:23** However it is not offered unconditionally, but people have to qualify to receive it. **The condition to receiving it is to believe in Christ as Lord and Savior**

> *"For God so loved the world, that he gave his one and only Son, that whoever believes in him should not perish, but have eternal life."* **John 3:16**

After believing in Christ, one is qualified also to be born of God

Bible Rap

> *"But as many as received him, to them he gave the right to become God's children, to those who believe in his name."* **John 1:12**

Upon believing, one is reckoned to be "in Christ" and is given the permanent indwelling of the Holy Spirit.

> *"in whom you also, having heard the word of the truth, the gospel of your salvation, — in whom, having also believed, you were sealed with the Holy Spirit of promise, who is a pledge of our inheritance, to the redemption of God's own possession, to the praise of his glory."* **Ephesians 1:13,14**

But what kind of believing is being spoken of here?

For there is a kind of believing that does not save.

James 2:14 (Rap)
My dear brothers, what does it gain
If one believes, but only in vain.
For if faith does not affect how he behaves,
I don't really think that kind of faith saves

There is also the example in the parable of the sower (Luke 8:4-15) of the seed that fell on the rock. Jesus says of these *"Those on the rock are they who, when they hear, receive the word with joy; but these have no root, <u>who believe for a while</u>, then fall away in time of temptation."* **Luke 8:13**

Becoming a Christian

Some fell on rocks but withered and died
For their faith was not deep enough to be qualified
To receive the life God promised to those
Who really believed Jesus died and arose.
Yes at first they were overjoyed
But when trials came their faith was destroyed
For they received it without their faith being rooted
And so fell away after they were persecuted

They did not have the kind of faith that qualifies them to receive salvation. Indeed there are even those whom in one sense are called "believers" but are "false brethren." In the book of Acts, with its historical emphasis, Luke records what people were called.

> **Acts 15:5** *But some of the sect of the Pharisees <u>who believed</u> rose up, saying, "It is necessary to circumcise them, and to charge them to keep the law of Moses."*

But in the book of Galatians, the apostle Paul records what they actually were. Speaking of the same people, he says:

> *"This was because of the <u>false brothers</u> secretly brought in, who stole in to spy out our liberty which we have in Christ Jesus, that they might bring us into bondage."*
> **Galatians 2:4**

However, all of these could legitimately be called

Bible Rap

"Christian." For the word "Christian" is only used three times in the Bible and all with reference to what the followers of Christ were called by outsiders without reference to their actual salvation status. And thus also concerning the New Testament letters written to the Christian churches, it is understood that Christians are not saved just because they associate themselves outwardly with a particular institution. Paul writes to the Corinthian Christians saying:

> *"Test your own selves, whether you are in the faith. Test your own selves. Or don't you know as to your own selves, that Jesus Christ is in you?—unless indeed you are disqualified."* **2Corinthians 13:5**

So what kind of faith does qualify one for salvation?

The faith that saves is characterized as a conviction. In describing saving faith, Paul points to Abraham's faith saying:

> *"Yet, looking to the promise of God, he didn't waver through unbelief, but grew strong through faith, giving glory to God, and <u>being fully assured</u> that what he had promised, he was able also to perform."* **Romans 4:20,21**

The faith that saves is that which is confident in the promise of God, fully assured which is also indicated by its inevitable perseverance.

> *"For we have become partakers of Christ, if we hold fast the beginning of our confidence firm to the end."* **Hebrews 3:14**

> *"By which (gospel) also you are saved, if you hold firmly the word which I preached to you—unless you believed in vain."* **1Co 15:2**

And by "full assurance" I am not speaking of a person feeling fully assured that they are saved. I am speaking of being fully assured that what God has promised he is able also to accomplish. The object of faith is not our own faith. The object of faith is the promise of God and the One behind that promise.

As with any conviction, the faith that saves is not one that simply says it believes, but rather it is also application oriented.

> *"Not everyone who says to me, 'Lord, Lord,' will enter into the Kingdom of Heaven; <u>but he who does the will of my Father who is in heaven</u>."* **Matthew 7:21**

James 2:18 (Rap)
Some say, "You have faith, I have deeds"
But don't you think where that leads?
Our faith is revealed by what we do
So if you have faith, you'll have deeds too!

James 2:24 (Rap)
Faith that works, that's the kind
that justifies a man, I find.

It is not a faith in works but a faith that works which is the kind that saves.

But how does one develop saving faith?

<u>Saving faith is developed in cooperation with God as one follows Jesus Christ</u>.

Upon hearing the gospel, many cannot decide to believe or not believe. For belief is not simply a function of the will. People should not be coerced into making statements of faith that they really haven't come to believe. Nor should they be presumed to be saved if it's clear that their faith is not yet of saving value. There is no technique or ritual that will automatically save those who don't have salvific faith.

However, a person can decide to seek God *"Ask, and it will be given you. Seek, and you will find. Knock, and it will be opened for you."* **Matthew 7:7** Many simply need time to get to know Jesus better before they can legitimately make any statement of faith. Jesus stands at the door and knocks. *"Behold, I stand at the door and knock. If anyone hears my voice and opens the door, then I will come in and eat with him, and he with me."* **Revelation 3:20** Yes, you can pray an experimental sort of prayer to open to the door.

And you can decide to follow Jesus. This gets a person on the path to salvation. They've left Egypt and entered the desert on their way to the promise land. This is the Seeking phase of the Salvation process.

Leaving Egypt

A person's decision to follow Christ as a seeker is likened to Israel's leaving Egypt and crossing the Red Sea. But this did not mean they would make it to the promise land. Paul applies this to Christians, writing:

> *"Now I would not have you ignorant, brothers, that our fathers were all under the cloud, and all passed through the sea; and were all baptized into Moses in the cloud and in the sea; and all ate the same spiritual food; and all drank the same spiritual drink. For they drank of a spiritual rock that followed them, and the rock was Christ. However with most of them, God was not well pleased, for they were overthrown in the wilderness."* **1Corinthians 10:1-5**

The crossing of the Red Sea can also be likened to John's Baptism. It is a baptism of repentance. A person decides to turn from the direction in which they were going and follow Jesus.

Wandering Through the Wilderness

After leaving Egypt, they entered the desert. Jesus

also showed the way by taking similar steps. He was first baptized by John in a baptism of repentance. Although John himself admitted that Jesus needed no such baptism. But Jesus replied to him *"Allow it now, for this is the fitting way for us to fulfill all righteousness."* **Matthew 3:15** For he was acting on behalf of mankind. *"Then Jesus was led up by the Spirit into the wilderness to be tempted by the devil."* **Matthew 4:1** This was also what Israel experienced. They were literally led by the Holy Spirit in the form of a cloud by day and a pillar of fire by night. And Jesus combated his tempter with verses taken from the book of Deuteronomy, which was also the same book given to Israel in the desert. One of the verses that Jesus quotes reveals some of the purpose of such a desert wandering that Israel faced.

> *"You shall remember all the way which Yahweh your God has led you these forty years in the wilderness, that he might humble you, to prove you, to know what was in your heart, whether you would keep his commandments, or not. He humbled you, and allowed you to hunger, and fed you with manna, which you didn't know, neither did your fathers know; that he might make you know that man does not live by bread only, but by everything that proceeds out of the mouth of Yahweh does man live."* **Deuteronomy 8:2,3**

Becoming a Christian

Dying in the Desert

The wilderness has two purposes, both related. It is a place in which God both develops and tests our faith until it is of salvific value or else until we die in the wilderness. Those who die in the wilderness (as 1Corinthians 10:1-5 indicates) may be likened to those who while still identifying themselves with the Christian community, never come to true faith in Christ and die as nominal Christians or reject the leading of the Holy Spirit in a permanent sense.

> *"For concerning those who were once enlightened and tasted of the heavenly gift, and were made partakers of the Holy Spirit, and tasted the good word of God, and the powers of the age to come, and then fell away, it is impossible to renew them again to repentance; seeing they crucify the Son of God for themselves again, and put him to open shame."* **Hebrews 6:4-6**

For there are those with only a surface knowledge of Christ, not knowing Him personally, and repent to a degree, but turn back and are condemned.

> *"For if, after they have escaped the defilement of the world through the <u>knowledge</u> of the Lord and Savior Jesus Christ, they are again entangled therein and overcome, <u>the last state has become worse with them than the first</u>. For it would be better for them not*

to have known the way of righteousness, than, after knowing it, to turn back from the holy commandment delivered to them. But it has happened to them according to the true proverb, 'The dog turns to his own vomit again,' and 'the sow that had washed to wallowing in the mire.'" **2Peter 2:20-22**

Here the word "knowing" is the Greek word "epignosis." "epi" refers to surface, and "gnosis" to knowledge. Such people only have a surface knowledge of Christ. The same Greek word is used in Hebrews 10.

"For if we sin willfully after we have received the <u>knowledge</u> of the truth, there remains no more a sacrifice for sins, but a certain fearful expectation of judgment, and a fierceness of fire which will devour the adversaries." **Hebrews 10:26,27**

And this is the same kind of warning Paul gave to the Corinthian Christians in 1Cor 10 above. But another aspect of the 2Peter 2:20,21 passage is that such people are characterized as behaving in accordance with their unregenerate nature. Though for those born of God it is written that *"Therefore if anyone is in Christ, he is a new creation. The old things have passed away. Behold, all things have become new."* **2Corinthians 5:17**, yet these others are not characterized as having such a new nature. John also writes more explicitly, but speaking in a lifestyle sense says:

> *"Whoever is born of God doesn't commit sin, because his seed remains in him; and he can't sin, because he is born of God. In this the children of God are revealed, and the children of the devil. Whoever doesn't do righteousness is not of God, neither is he who doesn't love his brother."* **1John 3:9,10**

And indeed speaking further on the behavior of those born of God says:

> *"For this is the love of God, that we keep his commandments. His commandments are not grievous. For whatever is born of God overcomes the world. This is the victory that has overcome the world: your faith."* **1John 5:3,4**

So there is a natural behavior associated with being born of God as there is a natural behavior associated with the unregenerate nature. Thus the wilderness experience is the struggle of those yet to be born of God as they are on the road to salvation coming to know Christ.

Developing Salvific Faith

In the process of developing salvific faith, the most essential character quality God develops in us is HUMILITY. Isaiah mentions of the qualities of a person that make one to be esteemed in the eyes of God:

Bible Rap

"To this man will I look, even to him who is poor and of a contrite spirit, and who trembles at my word." **Isaiah 66:2**

Humility leads to Conviction of Sin, which is necessary for us to recognize our need for salvation and for the grace of God. This leads to <u>accepting Jesus as our Savior</u>.

Humility also leads to Conviction that the Bible is God's Word, and as such we derive our life from it, meaning that we read it with a mindset of application and submission. This leads to us to <u>accepting Jesus as our Lord</u>.

Indeed interacting with the Word of God with such a mindset develops one's faith as it is written: *"faith comes by hearing, and hearing by the word of God."*

Romans 10:17

But what was the particular message given to Israel in the desert? They were given the Law of Moses, which are the first five books of the Bible.

"So that the law has become our tutor to bring us to Christ, that we might be justified by faith." **Galatians 3:24**

And how does it do that? Not as a means or source of justification, but rather by bringing conviction of sin.

"Because by the works of the law, no flesh will be justified in his sight. <u>For through</u>

the law comes the knowledge of sin."

Romans 3:20
This is necessary to recognize our need for salvation and the grace of God to redeem us. For a person cannot believe in a manner acceptable to God unless they first agree with God as to their corrupt, sinful, unholy state.

The Law also reveals God's justice. For it would be unjust for God to simply forgive sin without an appropriate penalty being paid. Yet that is an incorrect concept of God that some other religions have. Furthermore it reveals the depth of God's hatred of sin and the degree of His wrath even against what some might consider little things. This drives us to despair if we have not a Savior. But many will come to this realization when it's too late.

Categories of Seekers

There are seekers who have different areas of their faith needing development before they can enter the promise land. The following are a few types that come to mind.

The Legalistic Self Righteous

The Jews of Jesus' time generally fit in this category, as well as those today who feel they are morally superior to others or feel they come from a morally superior culture. Jesus and Paul had the same approach for such people. Humiliate them by challenging them with the Law.

> **Mark 10:17-19** *As he was going out into the way, one ran to him, knelt before him, and asked him, "Good Teacher, what shall I do that I may inherit eternal life?" Jesus said to him, "Why do you call me good?* ***No one is good except one—God****. You know the commandments: 'Do not murder,' 'Do not commit adultery,' 'Do not steal,' 'Do not give false testimony,' 'Do not defraud,' 'Honor your father and mother.'*

This man needed to understand that no one is good, and in particular that he was not a good person. He admitted to keeping the commandments. But he didn't understand that it was not only the letter that was to be kept, but also the spirit of it. So Jesus revealed his idolatrous greed by giving him another command. Those who reckon themselves to be good need to be humiliated. Paul also does the same to them in **Romans 2**.

The Lawless Licentious

These are those who acknowledge Jesus as Savior, reckoning themselves as sinners, but continue to callously live a lifestyle of sin. Essentially they reject the Lordship of Christ or give only verbal acknowledgement of Christ as Lord, which means little to God. These people need to come to understand God's hatred of sin and that the Salvation that Christ offers is not just the forgiveness of sins but also ultimately salvation from their own innate sinfulness. A couple of good verses for them might be:

> *"Or don't you know that the unrighteous will not inherit the Kingdom of God? Don't be deceived. Neither the sexually immoral, nor idolaters, nor adulterers, nor male prostitutes, nor homosexuals, nor thieves, nor covetous, nor drunkards, nor slanderers, nor extortioners, will inherit the Kingdom of God."* **1Corinthians 6:9,10**

> *"He who overcomes, I will give him these things. I will be his God, and he will be my son. But for the cowardly, unbelieving, sinners, abominable, murderers, sexually immoral, sorcerers, idolaters, and all liars, their part is in the lake that burns with fire and sulfur, which is the second death."* **Revelation 21:7,8**

The Experience Oriented Feelers

These are those who like to express their feelings. They speak of enjoying Christ or feeling the Holy Spirit's leading. But while this is a legitimate part of the Christian life, there are those who believe only in a Jesus that they feel and not in the Biblical Christ. Their Christ tends not be the Christ of the Bible, but rather a Christ made in their own image much as the people of Israel made the golden calf to worship at

Mount Sinai. They didn't patiently listen to the Word of God that Moses was bringing to them, but made an image of God they could control in accordance with their own passions. These tend to deny or put down the idea that God rationally communicated to us through the Bible and opt for a purely existentialistic attitude towards the Christian life. They are irrational experience seekers. This is New Age Existentialistic Christianity.

But God can work with that. These need to develop an appreciation of the promise of God and for the position in Christ that God offers. Believing God's promise is the focus of Biblical faith, not feeling a feeling. As such the concept of forgiveness of sins is rather foreign as it is a positional concept.

These people can also be weak on the idea of actually doing things other than expressing their feelings. For their emphasis is not on doing the Word, but on feeling. But the repentance the Bible speaks of is an honest attempt to change not only one's attitude, but one's behavior as well. A good verse for these people is

> **2Corinthians 5:7** *"for we walk by faith, not by sight."*

"Sight" includes "feelings" and related Charismatic experiences. Legitimate experiences of Christ should be viewed as secondary effects of believing and obeying Him, rather than being central to one's faith. Salvific faith is faith in Christ and not faith in one's own feelings.

The Do Nothing Thinkers

These are those who say they believe, but what they mean is that they merely understand. Yes they may have a right concept of the message. But the reality of the ideas has not set in. In contrast to the existentialistic Christians, these Christians don't have a sense of the reality of it all. And they may like to argue issues of armchair theology, but are not application oriented in their thinking. I mentioned some verses in James above, which are useful to them. Also:

James 1:22-25 (Rap)
Do the word, don't just be a hearer,
Like a man looking into a mirror.
He turns away, and yes he does
Forget what kind of man he was.
But if you look into the word with care,
Not forgetting what you hear,
And doing what it says to you,
You'll be blessed in what you do.

Also by the Holy Spirit, God helps to bring these into the reality of the message through experiences. We saw God doing miracles in the desert to provide food and drink for the Israelites and miraculously helping them to survive. With their cooperation, these kinds of evidences would help them to develop a genuine reliance upon God's grace, growing confidently of the reality of His presence and power to save.

The Jordan River Crossing

The writer of Hebrews speaks of the failure of Israel to enter into the promise land saying, *"To whom did he swear that <u>they wouldn't enter into his rest</u>, but to those who were **disobedient**? We see that they were not able to enter in **because of unbelief**."* **Hebrews 3:18,19**

Having been led all the way to the Jordan River and then refusing to cross, this kind of rejection is the final sin against the leading of the Holy Spirit which incurs a permanent rejection and condemnation of the unbeliever, as Hebrews 6:4-6 also indicates which I mentioned previously. But many are actually on the way towards the Jordan, having yet to come to a sufficient revelation of the gospel to make such a choice. As I said at the beginning, belief is not simply a matter of choice. However, having been given sufficient evidence, a choice is called for.

While the crossing of the Red Sea has been likened to John's baptism—a baptism of repentance, the crossing of the Jordan is likened to Christ's baptism—a baptism of regeneration. For John says, *"I baptized you in water, but he will baptize you in the Holy Spirit."* **Mark 1:8** This is what Jesus spoke of saying, *"Most assuredly, I tell you, unless one is <u>born anew</u>, he can't see the Kingdom of God."* **John 3:3** This is when one actually becomes a son of God. Jesus says, "I tell you the truth, no one can enter the kingdom of God unless he is born of water and the Spirit." Being born of water is one's physical birth, for *"That which is born of the flesh is flesh."* But being born of the Spirit is a second birth, a spiritual birth, for *"That which is born of the Spirit is spirit."* **John 3:6** So also there are two kinds of baptism. The one of repentance is in water. But the other of regeneration is in the fire of the Spirit.

Once one believes with salvific faith and decides to cross the Jordan, being born of God takes no effort at all on the person's part. It is completely accomplished apart from human effort, as it is written: *"But as many as received him, to them he gave the right to become God's children, to those who believe in his name: who were <u>born not of blood, nor of the will of the flesh, nor of the will of man, but of God</u>."* **John 1:12,13**

The Promise Land

Hebrews describes the promise land as a land of rest and likens it to the Sabbath rest saying, *"There remains therefore a Sabbath rest for the people of God. For he who has entered into his rest has himself also rested from his works, as God did from his."* **Heb 4:9,10** Those born of God rest in the grace of God, as it is written: *"Now when a man works, his wages are not credited to him as a gift, but as an obligation. However, to the man who does not work but trusts God who justifies the wicked, his faith is credited as righteousness."* **Romans 4:4,5** Such people have been transferred into a new kingdom.

"Giving thanks to the Father, who made us fit to be partakers of the inheritance of the saints in light; who delivered us out of the power of darkness, and translated us into the Kingdom of the Son of his love; in whom we have our redemption, the forgiveness of our sins." **Colossians 1:12-14**

And as the forgiveness of sins is a free gift, so also is salvation from one's own sinfulness, being experience to a degree in this life and ultimately in a permanent sense in the next. While striving to walk as Christ walked in this age, those born of God set their hopes on their future resurrection. For even Job declared:

"But as for me, I know that my Redeemer lives. In the end, he will stand upon the earth. After my skin is destroyed, then in my flesh shall I see God, Whom I, even I, shall see on my side. My eyes shall see, and not as a stranger. My heart is consumed within me." **Job 19:25-27**

Printed in the United States
49127LVS00001B/22-51